Vampire

Vampire

THE COMPLETE
GUIDE TO THE WORLD
OF THE UNDEAD

MANUELA DUNN-MASCETTI

VIKING
STUDIO
BOOKS

VIKING STUDIO BOOKS
Published by the Penguin Group
Viking Penguin, a division of Penguin Books USA Inc.,
375 Hudson Street, New York, NY 10014, U.S.A.
Penguin Books Ltd, 27 Wrights Lane
London W8 5TZ, England
Penguin Books Australia Ltd, Ringwood,
Victoria, Australia
Penguin Books Canada Ltd, 10 Alcorn Avenue, Suite 300,
Toronto, Ontario, Canada M4V 3B2
Penguin Books (N.Z.) Ltd, 182-190 Wairau Road,
Auckland 10, New Zealand

Penguin Books Ltd, Registered Offices:
Harmondsworth, Middlesex, England

First American Edition
Published in 1992 by Viking Penguin,
a division of Penguin Books USA Inc.

1 3 5 7 9 10 8 6 4 2

Produced by Labyrinth Publishing (UK) Ltd., London, England
Art direction and design by Ivor Claydon, London, England.

An earlier edition of this work was published in Great Britain as *Chronicles of the Vampire* by Bloomsbury
Publishing Ltd., 1991.

Library of Congress Cataloging in Publication Data

Mascetti, Manuela Dunn
Vampire : the complete guide to the world of the undead / by
Manuela Dunn Mascetti.
p. cm
ISBN 0-670-84664-3
1. Vampires. I. Title
GR830.V3M29   1992
398′. 45—dc20   92-53515

Printed by Mohndruck GmbH, Gutersloh, Germany.
Typeset by Goodfellow & Egan, London, England.

Contents

Introduction

The Doors to Darkness

The figure of the vampire, a creature clad in darkness and legend, who awakens at night and drinks the life substance of his victims in order to replenish his own, has haunted man's imagination for centuries. There is a wealth of material in the legends, hear-says, witness accounts, and true facts reported over the centuries to give fuel to a compulsive fascination with the horror of "the walking dead."

The fear of the vampire does not arise only from fantasy but frequently from substantial and documented reporting. Europe, and especially its eastern borders, was at times plagued by hordes of vampires who literally bled the population of medieval villages to death. The more precise investigations of science were summoned by local priests or the lords of the manor in attempts to put an end to the horrors perpetuated at night in their districts. The visiting scientists discovered that vampires had an extensive history and a clear lineage of their own and were not, as was previously thought, simply a local phenomenon. Their origins could in fact be traced to ancient Egyptian times when the cult and worship of the dead was ritually represented by ceremonies in which the acolytes revered a divinity that looked like a dark bird. This sinister bird represented the flight of the soul at the moment of death and its journey into the world of shadows. The dead, who were "alive" in their own world, occasionally came to plague the inhabitants of the world of light and sometimes even took them back into the unknown, stealing their lives away.

As Austrian troops took possession of the lands that lie in the eastern borders of Europe, parts of Serbia and Wallachia, the occupying forces began to notice and file reports on a peculiar local practice. The local population would exhume bodies in order to "kill" them. Literate outsiders began to attend such exhumations and write reports on what they saw. These witness accounts, perhaps sometimes distorted by fertile imaginations, filtered through into Austria, Germany, France, and England. The rest of Europe thus became aware of practices that were by no means of recent origin, but had simply been provided, for the first time, with effective "publicity" of "the strange goings-on in Transylvania." The Slavic *vampir*, or *upir* as it was sometimes called, found echo in similar creatures in Europe who were referred to in their own cultures by entirely different names. The fact that

Victorian vampirism was given a complex tone of sexual innuendo and baroque elegance by the literature of the time.

these phenomena were restricted not only to a small, barbaric area, but were also found everywhere else, gave credence to the *vampire* as we know him today. European scholars found cases of "undead" in far-off cultures such as China, Indonesia, and the Philippines. It seemed that vampires existed everywhere, and in a variety of cultures. The vampires were dead people who, having died before their time, not only refused to remain dead, but returned to bring death to their friends and neighbors.

Death brings death, a fond and most ancient belief and foundation to a host of complex and undeniable instincts. Modern man has long lost touch with his deeper intuitions – those dark, often emotional wells of understanding that are not associated with reason. The vampire, ancient and modern, is truly born from these regions of the unconscious with small and significant remnants surfacing to bring us intensely tantalizing hints, keeping our interest without ever providing the whole truth.

VAMPIRE – The Complete Guide to the World of the Undead, has grown from these dark hints and legends, gathered together over thousands of years, recorded in stories, accounts, and encounters that tell of the black angels that stalk the world, refusing to die. Information for the researcher is diffuse and secretive, often confusing, and tends to cast an unexpected sense of uncertainty over those who delve. Nothing precise can be delineated, nothing which gives the researcher reason to rationalize, only a deep sense of doubt – arguments with loved ones, premonitions of danger, dreams of fleeing or attacking monsters, and the tendency to live under a kind of shadow – the shadow that the vampire displays when he opens his cape for the victim to enter.

Thus the reader enters the *VAMPIRE – The Complete Guide to the World of the Undead* with this warning, for these pages contain the essence of the Princes of Darkness – the sense being that dust may lie upon the surfaces, that the book was taken from the library of Count Dracula himself, the arch collector, ultimately elegant and entirely dangerous. Look out for blood hidden with stealth between the lines of the legends – facts or fictions, who knows the difference? Perhaps there is none in this reality – and to "enjoy" this book is to enter just that reality.

Chapter 1

The Anatomy of a Vampire

What is a vampire? Is it a human being, and therefore a "he" or a "she," or truly an "it" – a monstrously evil and hideously ugly creature that happens to bear a human form? This dilemma between the recognizably human form and the possibility of its deterioration into a monstrous appearance is in fact one of the keys to the understanding of the "popularization" of vampires, both in the past centuries and today. The vampire's form, though we can see it to be human, is also available in a grotesquely distorted version, giving us the true horror of the contrast between soft human flesh and rotting death. The physical features are repulsive: long nails that curve like claws; skin showing deathly pallor, except when flushed after feeding; eyes often described as "dead" but nevertheless possessing a hypnotic stare; and rat-like fangs prepared for attack. The vampire is also psychologically repulsive: he is evil, devoid of any moral code; he stands outside – and therefore threatens – all normal society; he drinks blood; he kills without mercy; and, still worse, he is capable of the final and most inhuman of acts – transforming his victims into equally horrific creatures – a unilateral decision that no mere human under his power is strong enough to prevent.

The result of such transformation is ostensibly an ordinary man or woman who, through very strange rituals involving the exchange of blood, is endowed with immortality. But the quality of the vampire's immortality is tinged with the punishment that belongs to he who defies natural law. Vampires live "on the other side;" they are the dead who have chosen to live among the living, rather than ascend or descend to those places where all souls must rest before undertaking another life's journey. Their world is cold, dark, and lonely. The hand of death guides their every action, and it is a yoke they must bear forever. As we will see, it has been the living human's fondest desire to prevent the occurrence of the returning soul – to pave the way to rest for the dead. Even the headstones that we see in our local cemeteries everywhere in the world were originally intended simply to prevent the dead from sitting up!

For the vampire must kill, his duty being to bring evil to the communities of fair men, for he is the servant of she who is insatiable – "Mistress Death."

Vampires thus plague lost villages in the mountains or in marshlands, they roam around the darkness of forests, they take residence in abandoned castles, and nowadays their presence is felt even in harbors, construction sites, and other forbidden corners of the modern metropolis.

But mankind has built up quite a dossier of information and material surrounding the appearance of the vampire and his somewhat disgusting habits, and this process of collecting and gathering information was not simply an act of fascination, but one intended to aid the future sufferer of vampiric activity in his quest to rid himself of the plague thereof. Seeing the problem is half way to solving it.

There is therefore available to us ordinary mortals a great deal of information on how to recognize a vampire. Some items have become better known than others, presumably through greater use – for example, the fact that vampires fear severally the sun, crucifixes, and garlic; they cannot cross water; they sleep in coffins and prefer young virgins as their victims; they must always carry a little of their native soil wherever they go; they must always have an evil assistant to do their dirty work by day.

Other facts may be less familiar but should be paid close attention, for often the lesser-known is the greater in importance. Vampires also have the reputation of conniving secrecy concerning their own weaknesses. There are, for example, both male and female vampires; there are vampires who are visible and others who can change their shape at will; there are vampires who do not suck blood from their victims at all. Instead, they prefer to steal things that are perhaps more valuable to a human being, such as youth, hope, and love.

It may be that the vampire is so compelling precisely because he is so repellent. He works so powerfully on our imagination because he represents such a distortion of human nature, a reversal of everything normal. This is one of the weapons that the vampire uses to invite his victims to meet death and the process of transformation that will make them like him. He catches our imagination and lures us towards a path of despair that looks and feels deceptively attractive. This is his greatest skill, though, as we shall learn, he has many others.

It is for this very reason that men and women before us have written accounts of fearsome and strange encounters with vampires. To warn us of the dangers, to give us clues that will counteract the powerful force of vampire seductions. The following pages describe exactly the physical nature of vampires as found in those accounts. The research has been gathered from many and different parts of the world, across centuries, to give the reader the widest spectrum so that he may be warned, and thus saved.

Grave Discoveries

 long time before vampires filled the pages of romantic horror stories, such as Bram Stoker's *Dracula* and became so popular as to be portrayed in both fiction and movies, they are said to have plagued rural villages in those lost corners of eastern Europe such as the provinces of Hungary, Romania, and Transylvania. The popular depiction of a vampire, the one that is familiar to our imagination, is of a tall, very thin, aristocratic man. He is dressed in a black suit and a long, enveloping black cape. As a concession to his origin the outfit of the classic vampire may be a little dusty and worn-looking, – having seen better days – but he is essentially an elegant character who, at first glance, we might not discard out of hand. However, on slightly closer examination we find that his irksome smile reveals protuberant, exaggeratedly long, and extremely sharp canine teeth. His breath is foul; his nails long and crooked like the fangs of a beast; his complexion so pale he looks as if he has just arisen from the grave.

But is this how the vampires that are said to have haunted villages really looked? Not at all. In fact, for the sake of the watchful, it is now important to look at a very different form of vampire from our rather grotesque but essentially elegant movie character – one that stalked the country lanes and fields of the distant past – a creature that may still be present in our darker regions. The following are eyewitness reports and give us the very best sources of proof.

EYEWITNESS ACCOUNT I: PETER PLOGOJOWITZ

The story of Peter Plogojowitz dates back to 1725 and was witnessed by German military officials stationed in the village of Kisilova, in the Rahm District, now Slavia. Kisilova was actually in Serbia, although, because of the confused political situation of the time, it has often been reported as being part of Hungary.

Our subject, Peter Plogojowitz had died ten weeks past. He had been buried according to the Raetzian custom, a local religious ritual of the time. It was revealed that in this same village, during a period of a week, nine people, both old and young, had also died after suffering a 24-hour illness. Each of them had publicly declared, "that while they were yet alive, but on their death-bed, the above mentioned Plogojowitz, who had died ten weeks earlier, had come to them in their sleep, laid himself on them, and throttled them, so that they would have to give up the ghost."

Others who heard these reports were naturally very distressed by them, and their belief in the authenticity of them was strengthened even more by the fact that Peter Plogojowitz's wife, after saying that her husband had come to her and demanded his *opanki*, or shoes, had left the village of Kisilova.

> *And since with such people (which they call vampires) various are to be seen —*
> *that is, the body undecomposed, the skin, hair, beard, and nails growing — the*
> *subjects resolved unanimously to open the grave of Peter Plogojowitz and to see if*
> *such above-mentioned signs were really to be found on him. To this end they came*
> *here to me and, telling of these events, asked me and the local pope, or parish*
> *priest, to be present at the viewing. And although I at first disapproved, telling*
> *them that the praiseworthy administration should first be dutifully and humbly*
> *informed, and its exalted opinion about this should be heard, they did not want to*
> *accommodate themselves to this at all, but rather gave this short answer: I could*
> *do what I wanted, but if I did not accord them the viewing and the legal*

recognition to deal with the body according to their custom, they would have to leave house and home, because by the time a gracious resolution was received from Belgrade, perhaps the entire village – and this was already supposed to have happened in Turkish times – could be destroyed by such an evil spirit, and they did not want to wait for this.

The narrator goes on to say that,

Since I could not hold these people from the resolution they had made, either with good words or with threats, I went to the village of Kisilova, taking along the Gradisk pope, and viewed the body of Peter Plogojowitz, just exhumed, finding, in accordance with thorough truthfulness, that first of all I did not detect the slightest odor that is otherwise characteristic of the dead, and the body, except for the nose, which was somewhat fallen away, was completely fresh. The hair and beard – even the nails, of which the old ones had fallen away – had grown on him; the old skin, which was somewhat whitish, had peeled away, and a new one had emerged from it. The face, hands, and feet and the whole body were so constituted, that they could not have been more complete in his lifetime. Not without astonishment, I saw some fresh blood in his mouth, which, according to the common observation, he had sucked from the people killed by him. In short, all the indications were present that such people (as remarked above) are said to have. After both the pope and I had seen this spectacle, while people grew more outraged than distressed, all the subjects, with great speed, sharpened a stake – in order to pierce the corpse of the deceased with it – and put this at his heart, whereupon, as he was pierced, not only did much blood, completely fresh, flow also through his ears and mouth, but still other wild signs (which I pass by out of high respect) took place. Finally, according to their usual practice, they burned the often-mentioned body, in hic casu, to ashes of which I inform the most laudable Administration, and at the same time would like to request, obediently and humbly, that if a mistake was made in this matter, such is to be attributed not to me but to the rabble, who were beside themselves with fear.

Each of the investigative accounts concerning the instance of vampires that were documented during the medieval period of European history had to be sealed by either a local official or a doctor. The seals above have been reproduced from actual seals found on the reports on these pages.

This lengthy account, written in the style characteristic of bureaucratic eastern Europe of the eighteenth century, reveals that the vampire, Peter Plogojowitz, was an ordinary peasant of the village of Kisilova. Unfortunately, the account does not tell us anything about his personality or physical characteristics before his death, but it is quite clear from the description that he was not from aristocratic stock, nor was he wearing a long black cape and a black tuxedo in his coffin – hardly details that would have been overlooked.

The account illustrates quite clearly the difference, at least in appearance, between the fictional and the folkloric vampire. The former, as we have already described, is elegant, aristocratic, and eccentric, with the grotesque aspect of his nature only visible beneath the outer glamor at second glance. The latter is perhaps more treacherous still for he is very like you and me and to be found among us among the millions of people who inhabit the earth.

In pages of this book we will come across the photography of Simon Marsden, an Englishman who has specialized in the works of the undead. Traveling throughout the world, he has produced some of the most atmospheric material on this subject, including pictures of Dracula's castle itself.

———————•••———————

It seems important, therefore, to proceed to examine very carefully the characteristics of Peter Plogojowitz as described, so that we may become familiar with the vampire species in all its potential forms. We can start by examining, through extract from the authentic report, some classic motifs of vampirism.

1. It might seem, on closer examination of the quoted report, that vampirism occurs as an epidemic. Evidence of this arises from the fact that first Peter Plogojowitz died and that within a week of his death, nine people, both old and young, also died, in each case of a sudden 24-hour illness. Peter Plogojowitz is held responsible for the deaths of the other nine people, just as a victim of an epidemic illness, such as the plague, might have been held responsible for the deaths of his fellow villagers. In light of modern medicine we might dismiss such an idea right away, but maybe this is the mistake of "rational" man – always using "concrete" evidence when mystery is lurking just beneath the surface, eating away at certainty. To the peasant, always aware of magic, vampirism was an epidemic. One vampire caused another vampire, who in turn caused a third, and so on. If they didn't move fast to rid themselves of this plague, then all their neighbors and friends would go the same way, and the village would soon spread its infection to the town, to the country, and eventually the world would be populated by the walking dead. This must have been the ultimate fear of those subjected to such experiences as that of the presence of Peter Plogojowitz. This fear still exists in the mind and memory of mankind, evidenced by short stories such as Place of Meeting by Charles Beaumont (1953) and still more recent stories and movies depicting the presence of the living dead in various forms.

2. The vampire leaves his grave at night, appears before his victims and either sucks blood or strangles them. This kind of vampire is known to experts as the *ambulatory* type and is the most common vampire of all.

3. The body is said to be "completely fresh": the nose, however, has fallen in, although the hair, beard and nails have grown and new skin has formed under the old. This is an important characteristic of vampires: they do not appear dead when exhumed. On the contrary, they show signs of rejuvenation.

4. The body has no foul odor. But this may not necessarily be typical of vampirism. An eighteenth-century ecclesiast, Don Calmet, observed that "when they (vampires) have been taken out of the ground, they have appeared red, with their limbs supple and pliable, without worms or decay; but not without great stench." The stench of the body is an important aspect of the nexus between vampirism and the plague – as we said before, in European folklore vampires cause epidemics. Foul smells were commonly associated with disease, even with the cause of disease. It was not unreasonable to imagine that as corpses smelled bad, bad smells must be a cause of disease and death. In order to combat such smells, strong-smelling substances such as aromatic softwoods, juniper, and ash were introduced. Vampirism, therefore, was believed to be catching.

5. We should note perhaps the strongest evidence of Peter Plogojowitz's vampiric state – the fresh blood of victims still trickling from his mouth. Unless this was somehow planted there, it would seem hard to deny as a piece of clear proof. How many corpses manage to retain uncongealed blood on their bodies? In addition, his own blood was still fresh and uncongealed, thus also condemning him as a vampire.

6. We learn that when the villagers stake the vampire, he bleeds profusely – after several weeks in the grave. The "wild signs" that the author spares us details of probably imply that the corpse's penis was erect. The vampire is a sexual creature, and his sexuality is obsessive. In Yugoslavian legends, for example, when the vampire is not sucking blood, he is apt to wear out his widow with his attentions, so that she too pines away, much like his other victims. This also raises the question of whether the vampire's activities are always only those of blood sucking, or whether

his young female victims may also suffer rape.

We can draw the conclusion that Peter Plogojowitz was the first person in his village to catch a genuine case of vampirism and, by infecting others with it, made a place for himself in history.

We can use this first example then to begin our list of genuine vampiric "qualities" –

1. The power to create a kind of epidemic of blood lust among chosen individuals, both male and female.

2. Vampires appear "undead" in the grave: the skin is fresh and there is no evident *rigor mortis;* fresh blood still flows in their veins.

3. There appears to be evidence that the vampire also retains a strong sexual appetite and that this vigor exists even in the grave.

EYEWITNESS ACCOUNT II: VISUM ET REPERTUM

The following report is perhaps the most notable instance of vampirism in which a whole village is affected. The case was so serious that it finally attracted the attention of the authorities and led to the report being known to history as Visum et Repertum (Seen and Discovered). The story is mainly associated with a man named Arnod Paole who died as the result of a fall from a haywagon. His death would no doubt have gone unnoticed had it not been for the fact that he was subsequently exhumed, staked, and burned. The report, made some time after the event, is a most curious and fascinating document.

VISUM ET REPERTUM

After it had been reported that in the village of Medvegia the so-called vampires had killed some people by sucking their blood, I was, by high degree of a local Honorable Supreme Command, sent there to investigate the matter thoroughly, along with officers detailed for that purpose and two subordinate medical officers, and therefore carried out and heard the present inquiry in the company of the captain of the Stallath Company of haiduks (a type of soldier), Gorschiz Hadnack, the bariactar (standard-bearer) and the oldest haiduk of the village, as follows: who unanimously recount that about five years ago a local haiduk by the name of Arnod Paole broke his neck in a fall from a haywagon. This man had during his lifetime often revealed that, near Gossowa in Turkish Serbia, he had been troubled by a vampire, wherefore he had eaten from the earth of the vampire's grave and had smeared himself with the vampire's blood, in order to be free from the vexation he had suffered. In 20 or 30 days after his death some people complained that they were being bothered by this same Arnod Paole; and in fact four people were killed by him. In order to end this evil, they dug up this Arnod

---

The angels that guard over the dead in our graveyards often take on the atmosphere of the darkness they protect us from.

Paole 40 days after his death — this on the advice of their hadnack (soldier), who had been present at such events before; and they found that he was quite complete and undecayed, and that fresh blood had flowed from his eyes, nose, mouth, and ears; that the shirt, the covering, and the coffin were completely bloody; that the old nails on his hands and feet, along with the skin, had fallen off, and that new ones had grown; and since they saw from this that he was a true vampire, they drove a stake through his heart, according to their custom, whereby he gave an audible groan and bled copiously. Thereupon they burned the body the same day to ashes and threw these into the grave. These people say further that all those who were tormented and killed by the vampire must themselves become vampires. Therefore they disinterred the above-mentioned four people in the same way. Then they also add that this Arnod Paole attacked not only the people but also the cattle, and sucked out their blood. And since the people used the flesh of such cattle, it appears that some vampires are again present here, inasmuch as, in a period of three months, 17 young and old people died, among them some who, with no previous illness, died in two or at the most three days. In addition, the haiduk Jowiza reports that his step-daughter, by name of Stanacka, lay down to sleep 15 days ago, fresh and healthy, but at midnight she started up out of her sleep with a terrible cry, fearful and trembling, and complained that she had been throttled by the son of a haiduk by the name of Milloe, who had died nine weeks earlier, whereupon she had experienced a great pain in the chest and became worse hour by hour, until finally she died on the third day. At this we went the same afternoon to the graveyard, along with the often-mentioned oldest haiduks of the village, in order to cause the suspicious graves to be opened and to examine the bodies in them, whereby, after all of them had been dissected, there was found:

1. A woman by the name of Stana, 20 years old, who had died in childbirth two months ago, after a three-day illness, and who had herself said, before her death, that she had painted herself with the blood of a vampire, wherefore both she and her child — which had died right after birth and because of a careless burial had been half eaten by the dogs — must also become vampires. She was quite complete and undecayed. After the opening of the body there was found in the **cavitate** pectoris *a quantity of fresh extravascular blood. The* vasa *(vessels) of the* arteriae *and* venae, *like the* ventriculis ortis, *were not, as is usual, filled with coagulated blood, and the whole* viscera, *that is, the* pulmo *(lung),* hepar *(liver),* stomachus, lien *(spleen),* et intestina *were quite fresh as they would be in a healthy person. The uterus was however quite enlarged and very inflamed externally, for the placenta and lochia had remained in place, wherefore the same was in complete* putredine. *The skin on her hands and feet, along with the old nails, fell away on their own, but on the other hand completely new nails were evident, along with a fresh and vivid skin.*

2. *There was a woman by the name of Miliza (60 years old), who had died after a three-month sickness and had been buried 90-some days earlier. In the chest much liquid blood was found, and the other viscera were, like those mentioned before, in a good condition. During her dissection, all the haiduks who were standing around marveled greatly at her plumpness and perfect body, uniformly stating that they had known the woman well, from her youth, and that she had, throughout her life, looked and been very lean and dried up, and they emphasized that she had come to this surprising plumpness in the grave. They also said that it was she who started the vampires this time, because she had eaten of the flesh of those sheep that had been killed by the previous vampires.*

3. *There was an eight-day-old child which had lain in the grave for 90 days and was similarly in a condition of vampirism.*

4. *The son of a haiduk, 16 years old, was dug up, having lain in the earth for nine weeks, after he had died from a three-day illness, and was found like the other vampires.*

5. *Joachim, also the son of a haiduk, 17 years old, had died after a three-day illness. He had been buried eight weeks and four days and, on being dissected, was found in similar condition.*

6. *A woman by the name of Ruscha who had died after a ten-day illness and had been buried six weeks previous, in whom there was much fresh blood not only in the chest but also in* **fundo ventriculi.** *The same showed itself in her child, which was 18 days old and had died five weeks previously.*

7. *No less did a girl ten years of age, who had died two months previously, find herself in the above-mentioned condition, quite complete and undecayed, and had much fresh blood in her chest.*

8. *They caused the wife of the Hadnack to be dug up, along with her child. She had died seven weeks previously, her child – who was eight weeks old – 21 days previously, and it was found that both mother and child were completely decomposed, although earth and grave were like those of the vampires lying nearby.*

9. *A servant of the local corporal of the haiduks, by the name of Rhade, 23 years*

On the previous pages we sample the power of a Simon Marsden picture representing death and decay. And above – this picture brings to mind the words of the French philosopher Jacques Lacan – "The mirror might reflect a little longer before returning an image to its owner."

old, died after a three-month-long illness, and after a five week burial was found completely decomposed.

10. The wife of the local bariactar, along with her child, having died five weeks previously, were also completely decomposed.

11. With Stanche, a local haiduk, 60 years old, who had died six weeks previously, I noticed a profuse liquid blood, like the others, in the chest and stomach. The entire body was in the oft-named condition of vampirism.

12. Milloe, a haiduk, 25 years old, who had lain for six weeks in the earth, also was found in the condition of vampirism mentioned.

13. Stanoika, the wife of a haiduk, 20 years old, died after a three-day illness and had been buried 18 days previously. In the dissection I found that she was in her countenance quite red and of a vivid color, and, as was mentioned above, she had been throttled, at midnight, by Milloe, the son of the haiduk, and there was also to be seen, on the right side under the ear, a bloodshot blue mark, the length of a finger. As she was being taken out of the grave, a quantity of fresh blood flowed from her nose. With the dissection I found, as mentioned often already, a regular fragrant fresh bleeding, not only in the chest cavity, but also in **ventriculo cordis.** *All the viscera found themselves in a completely good and healthy condition. The hypodermis of the entire body, along with the fresh nails of hands and feet, was as though completely fresh. After the examination had taken place, the heads of the vampires were cut off by the local gypsies and burned along with the bodies, and then the ashes were thrown into the river Morava. The decomposed bodies, however, were laid back into their own graves.*

Such an account could more easily have been written within the pages of a work of horror fiction. But this and many more such reports, signed and witnessed by local and even city officials and doctors, have formed the very real basis for beliefs in vampirism. These events, even though well-hidden within the yellowing pages of history books, are true as far as any historic event can be proven. They also created a very real and horrific fascination for the cultured ear of the romantic spirit that pervaded Europe at the time. It is easy to imagine the speculation, the elaboration, the transformation of such truths and their catalytic effect on audiences eager to shiver with fear at monstrous creatures who daunted far-away lands.

As before, we can take account of the various useful observations inherent in this examination of the events, and see if they add to our list of characteristics. We can observe first of all, an overall attitude from authorities involved in the investigation which might today be applied to, for example, a road accident or serious local epidemic. The whole matter is taken completely seriously.

1. The situation clearly causes extreme havoc in the local area and is not simply a small event passed by without much concern.

2. In two instances (Arnod Paole and Stana) people are said to have used the blood of the vampire as an antidote to vampirism. In both cases the remedy appears to have failed. From where does this "method" arise?

3. People complain that the dead Arnod Paole is terrorizing them at night.

4. The disinterment takes place 40 days after Paole's death. According to medical evidence the body should not be intact at this point. It is, however, found undecayed, his blood is fresh, and his hair and nails have continued to grow after death.

5. Paole's body is staked and then cremated. Note that the corpse groans and bleeds. The officials, unfortunately, do not witness this directly, but it is noted nevertheless as hear-say.

6. The victims of the vampire are said to become vampires themselves.

7. The vampire also attacks cattle. Those who eat the flesh of the cattle also become vampires.

8. Stana's child, who is buried carelessly, is dug up by dogs. This is a revealing

It is easy to see how the legends of the distant past maintain their power in the human mind, once etched in stone.

piece of information in so far as the introduction of the coffin was brought about by fears of vampirism (among other reasons) – that the body would accidentally be dug up by animals and would therefore not achieve departure from this life successfully, thus becoming vulnerable to vampirism.

9. In one of the examples of exhumation, that of Miliza, a body has not remained unchanged but is described as having become plump, whereas before death she was lean. This is an important fact, because, as we shall discover later, quite different, even contradictory conditions, are believed to indicate vampirism.

10. To provide proof that the undecayed bodies are unusual, it is noted, by contrast, that the other bodies have decayed naturally.

11. One vampire (Stanoika) had a mark under the ear. Fluekinger takes this as evidence of "throttling," but since it was customary to look for such a mark on the skin of a witch or vampire, this finding would have further confirmed the belief that something unnatural was occurring within the body.

We saw a rather different and quite tragic scene on the same island occasioned by one of those corpses that are believed to return after their burial. The one of whom I shall give an account was a peasant of Mykonos, naturally sullen and quarrelsome – a circumstance to be noted concerning such matters. He had been killed in the fields, no one knew by whom nor how. Two days after he had been buried in a chapel in the town, it was bruited about that he had been seen walking during the night taking long strides; that he came into houses and turned over furniture, extinguished lamps, embraced people from behind, and played a thousand little roguish tricks. At first people only laughed, but the matter became serious when the most respectable people began to complain. Even the popes acknowledged the fact, and doubtless they had their reasons. People did not fail to have masses said, but the peasant continued his little escapades without mending his ways. After a number of meetings of the town leaders and of the priests and monks, they concluded that it would be necessary – in accord with I don't know what ancient ceremony – to wait till nine days after the burial.

On the tenth day they said a mass in the chapel where the body lay, in order to

The appreciation of death, in such gruesome detail, has been lost down the ages.

drive out the demon that they believed to be concealed in it. The body was disinterred after the mass, and they set about the task of tearing out its heart. The butcher of the town, quite old and very maladroit, began by opening the belly rather than the chest. He rummaged about for a long time in the entrails, without finding what he sought, and finally someone informed him that it was necessary to cut into the diaphragm. The heart was torn out to the admiration of all the bystanders. But the body stank so terribly that incense had to be burned, but the smoke, mixed with the exhalations of this carrion, did nothing but increase the stench, and it began to inflame the minds of these poor people. Their imagination, struck by the spectacle, filled with visions. They took it into their heads to say that a thick smoke was coming from the body, and we did not dare say it was incense. People kept calling out nothing but "Vrykolakas!" in the chapel and in the square before it, this being the name they give to these supposed revenants. The noise spread through the streets as if it were being roared, and this name seemed to be invented to shake the vault of the chapel. Several of the bystanders claimed that the blood of this unfortunate man was quite red, and the butcher swore that the body was still warm, from which they concluded that the deceased had the severe defect of not being quite dead, or, to state it better, of letting himself be reanimated by the devil, for that is exactly the idea they have of a vrykolakas. They caused this name to resound in an astonishing manner. And then there arrived a crowd of people who professed loudly that they had plainly seen that the corpse had not become stiff, when they carried it from the fields to the church to bury it, and that as a result it was a true vrykolakas. That was the refrain.

I do not doubt that they would have maintained that the body did not stink, if we had not been present, so stunned were these poor people from the business, and so persuaded of the return of the dead. As for us, who had placed ourselves near the cadaver to make our observations as closely as possible, we almost perished from the great stench that emerged from it. When they asked us what we thought of the deceased, we answered that we thought him quite adequately dead. But because we wanted to cure – or at least not to irritate their stricken imagination – we represented to them that it was not surprising if the butcher had perceived some warmth in rummaging about in the entrails, which were putrefying; that it was not extraordinary if fumes were emitted, just as such emerge from a dung heap when one stirs it up; and as for the pretended red blood, it was still evident on the hands of the butcher that this was nothing but a stinking mess.

After all our reasoning, they were of a mind to go to the seashore and burn the heart of the deceased, who, in spite of this execution became less docile and made more noise than ever. They accused him of beating people at night, of breaking in doors, and even roofs; of breaking windows, tearing up clothes, and emptying pitchers and bottles. He was a very thirsty dead man: I believe that he did not spare any house but that of the consul, with whom we lodged. However, I have never viewed anything so pitiable as the state of this island. Everyone's head was turned: the wisest people were struck like the others. It was a regular illness of the brain, as dangerous as madness or rage. One saw entire families abandon their houses and come from the outlying areas of the town into the square, carrying their pallets, to pass the night there. Everyone complained of some new insult, and there were nothing but groans at the coming of night. The most intelligent ones withdrew to the country.

In so general a prepossession, we chose not to say anything. They would have treated us not just as fools but as infidels. How is one to bring an entire population back to its sense? Those who believed in their soul that we doubted the truth of the matter, came to us to reproach us for our incredulity and claimed to prove, by authoritative passages from the *Shield of Faith* of Pere Richard, a Jesuit missionary — that there was such a thing as a vrykolakas. He was a Latin, they said, and therefore you should believe him. Nor should we have got anywhere by denying the conclusion. They made a scene every morning, by the faithful recitation of the new jests committed by this night-bird, who was even accused of having committed the most abominable sins.

Those citizens who were most zealous for the public good believed that the most essential part of the ceremony had been deficient. The mass should not have been said, according to them, until after the heart of this unfortunate man had been torn out. They maintained that, with this precaution, the devil could not have failed to *have been surprised, and that without a doubt he would not have returned. Whereas in starting with the mass, they said, he had had all the time necessary to flee and to come back afterward to his convenience.*

After all these reasonings, they found themselves in the same difficulty as the first day. They meet night and day, debate, and organize processions for three days and three nights. They oblige the popes to fast, and one sees them running among the houses, the aspergillum in their hand, sprinkling holy water and washing the doors with it. With it they even filled the mouth of this poor vrykolakas.

We said so often to the administrators of the town that in a similar situation, in Christendom, one would not fail to establish a watch at night to observe what would happen in the town, that finally they arrested a few vagabonds who certainly had had a hand in these disorders. But apparently they were either not the principal agents, or else they were released too soon, for two days later, to make up for the fast they had undergone in prison, they began again to empty the jugs of wine of those who were so foolish as to leave their houses during the night. Whereupon people were obliged to take recourse again to prayer.

One day, as they recited certain prayers, after having planted I don't know how many naked swords in the grave of the corpse — which they disinterred three or four times a day, according to the caprice of whomever came by — an Albanian, who happened to find himself in Mykonos, took it upon himself to say, in a professional tone, that it was extremely ridiculous to use the swords of Christians in such a case as this. Can you not see, you poor blind people, he said, that the guard of these swords, forming a cross with the handle, prevents the devil from leaving this corpse! Instead, why don't you rather use Turkish sabers? The opinion of this clever man was of no use: the vrykolakas did not appear to be any more tractable, and everyone was in a strange dismay. They didn't know which saint to call upon, but with one voice, as though they had given one another the word, they began to cry out, throughout the village, that they had waited too long — it was necessary to burn the vrykolakas entirely. After that they defied the devil to return to set up quarters there. It was better to resort to such an extreme than to have the island deserted. And in fact there were already entire families who were packing up,

The elements that have been brought to bear on vampire lore over the centuries
are many and varied. They all relate to potential death, usually of an unpleasant
nature. And yet death is unknown to us in truth so we tend to accept anything
into vampiric legend that is ultimately frightening. Why, for example, does
almost every visit to a fictional vampire's castle result in major thunderstorms,
lightning and heavy rain?

---

*with the intention of retiring to Syra or Tinos. So then they carried the vrykolakas,
by the order of the administrators, to the tip of Saint George's Island, where a
great funeral pyre had been prepared, with tar, out of fear that the wood, as dry as
it was, would not burn fast enough for them on its own. The remains of this
unfortunate cadaver were thrown on and consumed in a short time (this was the
first of January, 1701). We saw the fire as we returned from Delos. You could call it
a true fire of rejoicing, for one no longer heard the complaints against the
vrykolakas. They were content to observe that the devil had certainly been caught
this time, and they composed a few songs to ridicule him.*

*In the whole archipelago people are persuaded that it is only the Greeks of the
Orthodox Church whose corpses are reanimated by the devil. The inhabitants of
the island of Santorini are terribly afraid of such types of werewolves, and the
people of Mykonos, after their visions had dissipated, were equally afraid of
prosecution by the Turks and by the bishop of Tinos. Not a single pope wanted to
be present at Saint George when they burned the body, out of fear that the bishop
would exact a sum of money for their having exhumed and burned the deceased
without his permission. As for the Turks, it is certain that, at their first visit, they
did not fail to make the community of Mykonos pay for the blood of this poor
devil, who became in every way an abomination and horror to his country.*

Beyond The Physical

he most remarkable feature of a vampire is that, though his appearance is human, he has little in common with other men. This strangely enigmatic fact gives the vampire probably his or her greatest power over mere mortals who naturally possess a passion that is aroused by fugitive beauty, by something that appears real and yet is not; the power of a creature which is in effect a "human" illusion.

Vampires have chosen to live among us exactly *because* we seem to be obsessed by that which we cannot possess, *because* we long to attain the impossible, *because* we fulfil our desires, fears, and expectations – the vacuum in our lives, with what they represent. One could even go so far as to argue that a vampire is a perfectly polished mirror on which we project all our dreams and fancies, sexual and intellectual, and the projection endows this strange creature with an attraction we find impossible to resist.

In order to understand the subtle power that vampires exercise over our psyche, we can first meditate upon the tales of men who were ruined by them, whose lives, loves, souls, and hearts were stolen by these evil creatures of darkness.

> *He gazed upon the mirth around him, as if he could not participate therein.*
> *Apparently, the light laughter of the fair only attracted his attention, that he might*
> *by a look quell it, and throw fear into those breasts where thoughtlessness reigned.*
> *Those who felt this sensation of awe, could not explain whence it arose: some*
> *attributed to the dead gray eye, which, fixing upon the object's face, did not seem to*
> *penetrate and at one glance pierce through to the inward workings of the heart; but*
> *fell upon the cheek with a leaden ray that weighed upon the skin it could not pass.*

The movie world has enhanced our mythological past with mysterious horror.
Frederic March in the 1932 version of *Dr Jekyll and Mr Hyde*.

This passage was extracted from Dr. John Polidori's (1795–1821) famous tale *The Vampyre*. Dr. Polidori was the uncle of the future Dante Gabriel and Christina Rossetti and was the youngest man to be awarded a medical degree by the University of Edinburgh. He was also the travel companion to George Gordon, Lord Byron (1788–1824), the great English romantic writer and poet. In 1816 Lord Byron planned a trip across Europe, intending to visit Switzerland, where he would meet with his friends Percy Bysshe Shelley and his wife, Mary Shelley. Polidori was selected partly because it was customary to bring along a doctor on such journeys, and partly because of his bright and engaging conversation. But the two men quarreled often during the trip, and the tension was high when they reached Geneva and were united with the Shelleys. During a period of nasty weather, the group, to pass the time, began reading some volumes of ghost stories translated from German into French. One day, inspired by the gloom reflected on the stormy waters of Lake Geneva, Byron announced that each would write a ghost story. Mary Shelley dreamed up the idea for her novel Frankenstein, which she began at once. Percy Shelley lost interest quickly in the project and wrote nothing. Lord Byron wrote a brief fragment of a story in his notebook. The quarrels between Polidori and Byron continued and eventually the doctor left Geneva. In 1819 a story entitled *The Vampyre* was published in the New Monthly Magazine and was attributed to Lord Byron. The next month's issue, however, contained a letter from Dr. Polidori in which he claimed the story as his own, though he admitted that it was based on the fragments that Byron had begun writing and had abandoned in Geneva. The main character, Lord Ruthven, is apparently based on Lord Byron himself and it offers us many clues as to the intriguing nature of a vampire.

Aubrey, John Polidori's alter-ego in the story, is spell-bound by Lord Ruthven (alias Lord Byron) and decides to observe him closely:

He watched him; and the very impossibility of forming an idea of the character of a man entirely absorbed in himself, who gave few other signs of his observation of external objects, than the tacit assent to their existence, implied by the avoidance of their contact: allowing his imagination to picture every thing that flattered its

Byron (left) and Mary Shelley (below), two of the midwives of nineteenth century literary vampirism.

Byron's pedigree was a fake however, for his greatest work of vampirism was written by Polidori.

propensity to extravagant ideas, he soon formed this object into the hero of a romance, and determined to observe the offspring of his fancy, rather than the person before him.

This is the first dangerous step into the web that covers the entrance to the vampire's domain: since the creature appears to be "entirely absorbed in himself," and since there appears to be no basis for character or personality to anchor any perception of the vampire, then the human mind begins to elaborate, to build upon reality with fantasy – the object (the vampire) becoming "the hero of a romance."

The second step into the vampire's web is the desire of the human mind to believe in its offspring, or a similar creature to itself, rather than in the reality which it faces; in other words, we prefer to believe in what we create in our fantasies, rather than in what we perceive with our senses. Thus the vampire appears empty, like a shadow, and we, the human observers, may project whatever form will grip our imagination most, truly believing that *this* is the vampire. In this complex and disturbing fashion the process of depletion begins, and through this balance of fantasy and reality the vampire sucks not only blood, but the psychic energy which controls our mental and physical functions, slowly but surely becoming a perfect projection of our desires.

In folklore, drawn from tales such as those we have read, the vampire is very different from his fictional counterpart. His color is never pale, as one would expect from a corpse. His face is commonly described as florid, or of a healthy color, and this may be attributed to his "drinking" habits. "The limbs remain flexible, the body is undamaged and swollen up and can give forth fresh blood, the face is red from the blood he drunk . . . the eyes are open." We note here that the presence of blood, especially at the lips, may be one of the reasons for the association between vampires and the plague. The pneumonic form of the plague causes the victim to expel blood from the mouth, and the combination of visible blood with unexpected and quite sudden deaths may have led to the belief that vampirism was responsible for the disease.

In some witness accounts we find that the reporters note a peculiarity in the teeth of the vampires, ". . . the lips which are markedly full and red and are drawn back from the teeth which gleam long, sharp, as razors, and ivory white." It is also a popular belief in eastern Europe that children born with teeth are destined to become vampires. In particular peculiarity, the folkloric and the fictional vampires are similar, for they are both believed to use their teeth to extract blood from their victims.

But for all the differences between the appearance in the grave of fictional and folkloric vampires, there is one notable similarity: when found in their graves, both lie quietly in a kind of trance, awaiting their fate. They are not dangerous in this condition, at least until attacked. Their trance points to their non-human nature more than all the physical signs examined so far in this book. There is more to the physiology of a vampire than we have hitherto seen. The creature thus far revealed seems all too physical, but the real vampire possesses characteristics that go beyond the physical nature observed by official witnesses, possessing traits that can only be studied upon embarking on a still more intimate relationship.

> *Lord Ruthven in his carriage, and amidst the various wild and rich scenes of nature, was always the same: his eyes spoke less than his lip; and though Aubrey was near the object of his curiosity, he obtained no greater gratification from it than the constant excitement of vainly wishing to break that mystery, which to his exalted imagination began to assume the appearance of something supernatural.*

Audrey observes that Lord Ruthven "was profuse in his liberality," though his charitable nature was somewhat questionable since he gave riches to the idle, the vagabond, and the beggar, whilst he turned away the virtuous with sneers of disdain, even though they may have fallen in misfortune. Whenever someone knocked at his door asking for something, "not to relieve his wants, but to allow him to wallow in his lust, or to sink him still deeper in his iniquity, he was sent away with rich charity." Lord Ruthven's generosity was, however, of a very sinister nature for "all those upon whom it was bestowed, inevitably found that there was a curse upon it, for they were all either led to the scaffold, or sunk to the lowest and the most abject misery."

Lord Ruthven brought the same malice to his relationships with women: all those women who he had sought, apparently for their virtue, had since his departure, "thrown even the mask aside, and had not scrupled to expose the whole deformity of their vices to the public gaze."

Lord Ruthven, the "vampyre," is a master of psychological manipulation. He plays upon the lust of the wretched by giving them more, so that they end up beyond redemption from vice, and in his intimate relationships with women he has the power to transform even the most virtuous into a shamelessness. But who could resist his power? The vampire in John Polidori's story appears in classical disguise: a cultured and mannered man of great sophistication and lineage (a lord, no less), a hazy but nevertheless interesting background, and such charisma that few avoid subjugation to it. He spoke of himself as an individual with no sympathy for any other being on the crowded earth, save those to whom he addressed himself, from whom he intended to take, rather than give.

This style of vampire must be the very worst and most cunning of creatures – knowing so well how to use the serpent's art to gain the greatest affection and the deepest trust from those who would be their victims.

In the tale *A Mysterious Stranger* (anonymous, 1860) the vampire describes himself to a party of five horsemen headed by the Knight of Fahnenberg. They had been riding across the Carpathian Mountains to take possession of a castle and lands left in inheritance to the Knight by a childless brother. As evening approached Boreas, a fearful northwest wind raged into a powerful storm over the region. Amid the gusts of wind the party could hear the howling of wolves. They were informed by an attendant, who guided them towards their final destination, that at the edge of the wood they were crossing there lay a lake where a pack of fierce wolves dwelt. These wolves had been known to kill even the great bears of the mountains. The howls could be heard more distinctly and closer to the riders than before, and soon they were able to see the eyes of the beasts sparkling in the forest. The party struggled against the raging storm to reach the end of the wood and sought shelter in the castle of Klatka, which was said to be haunted. Suddenly, just as the Knight

The modern atmosphere that surrounds vampirism derives from many centuries
of the human fear of death, but laced also with an elegance and beauty that is
reflected in the graveyard statue above, shot in Transylvania.

and his companions were about to be eaten by the wolves before they could enter the castle gates, a stranger leapt from the shadow of an oak tree and, with a few strides, placed himself between the party and the wolves. As soon as the stranger appeared the wolves gave up their pursuit, tumbled over each other, and set up a fearful howl. The stranger raised his hand, waved it, and the wild animals crawled back into the thickets like a pack of beaten hounds. Without casting a glance at the travelers, who were too much overcome by astonishment to speak, the stranger walked up the castle path and disappeared.

Once the Knight and his companions reached their destination and had settled in the castle, they began to explore the region on horseback and happened to come to castle Klatka. Here they met the stranger, whom they thanked for having saved them from the wolves. He claimed that the beasts were afraid of him. In order to demonstrate their gratefulness, the Knight invited the stranger to visit them at their new home. The stranger seemed reticent to meet with people and replied, ". . . besides, I generally remain at home during the day; it is my time for rest. I belong, you must know, to that class of persons who turn day into night, and night into day, and who love everything uncommon and peculiar."

However, a few days later, he presented himself at the Knight's castle in time for supper, when everyone could see him in full view in the brilliantly lit dining chamber,

> *He was a man of about forty, tall, and extremely thin. His features could not be termed uninteresting – there lay in them something bold and daring – but the expression was on the whole anything but benevolent. There were contempt and sarcasm in the cold gray eyes, whose glance, however, was at times so piercing that no one could endure it long. His complexion was even more peculiar than his features: it could neither be called pale nor yellow; it was a sort of gray, or, so to speak dirty white, like that of an Indian who has been suffering long from fever; and was rendered still more remarkable by the intense blackness of his beard and short cropped hair. The dress of the unknown was knightly, but old-fashioned and neglected; there were great spots of rust on the collar and breastplate of his armor;*

and his dagger and the hilt of his finely worked sword were marked in some places with mildew.

From these descriptions we get an idea of the non-human qualities of a vampire: a certain detachment from both worldly concerns and human beings; a hardened will which compels him to mock life and all good and virtuous things; the hypnotic stare; the manipulation of feelings and of the psyche; the allurement of victims into an evil world of darkness. These are characteristics which we do not generally meet in everyday life, and whenever a stranger displays them to us we must put our souls on the alert and avoid the alluring vampire's trap which leads to one certainty alone – death.

Chapter 2
Birth of the Undead

Now we take a closer look at how a vampire is born. We know from evidence already set out that these creatures were originally human before undergoing an unique process of transformation – that the vampire body is dead, but remains, mysteriously, active, continuing to function for many years, even centuries, unless "killed" again. We also know that the victims of vampires become vampires themselves – that vampirism is catching, even epidemic, like the plague itself.

But this is not the whole story. There are still unanswered questions. For example, are there prerogatives to vampirism – so to speak "unnatural" rules laid down by existence that dictate that only certain kinds of victims are chosen to become vampires. Or can any one of us become transformed? And if a vampire feeds on the blood of humans, do all his victims – of which there must be many – become vampires, too, or is there a selection process at work?

The answers to these questions are somewhat confused by the fact that vampires are extremely shrewd and crafty creatures – unwilling to be "caught in the act" of sinking those razor-sharp canines into the victim's jugular. On the few occasions that first-hand witnesses were able to swear their presence at a confrontation between vampire and victim, the main emphasis was on killing the vampire, rather than examining the causes and reasons for the event. In some instances we cannot be sure whether it was the spirit of the dead person which terrorized the community at night and brought death to others, or whether it was the body that came out of the grave, killed at night, and returned to its coffin before dawn. In the eyewitness accounts examined in the previous chapter, we find no remarks on the state of the coffins, whether, for instance, they had been broken open, and since the main witnesses, the victims, are all dead, much of our evidence remains circumstantial.

The best account of the birth of a vampire is given in Anne Rice's exceptional book *Interview with the Vampire*. This extraordinarily detailed account satisfies our thirst for answers and gives a good account of the process occurring in the physical body during transformation. This metamorphosis leaves behind all the physical laws that govern humanity in ordinary life and adopts new ones that permit it to live outside time and physical deterioration.

In the book, the vampire Louis tells his tale of initiation to a young journalist, in present day America. He declares that he was made into a vampire at the age of 25 in the year 1791. A terrible tragedy has occurred within Louis's family, for which he feels responsible; he is haunted by guilt and loses faith in life and in himself.

> *I drank all the time and was at home as little as possible. I lived like a man who wanted to die but who had no courage to do it himself. I backed out of two duels more from apathy than cowardice and truly wished to be murdered. And then I was attacked. It might have been anyone – and my invitation was open to sailors, thieves, maniacs, anyone. But it was a vampire.*

The vampire drains Louis's blood almost to the point of death. The monstrous creature then returns after a few nights, and Louis is so weakened that at first he mistakes him for yet another doctor. But as soon as the vampire's face is visible in the light of the lamp, Louis recognizes that he is no ordinary human being.

Craig Hall in Perthshire, seen from the deep dark forests that lie thickly carpeted below, evoke scenes from Bram Stoker's *Dracula*, in which the terrible Count intended to take up residence in the British Isles. Such a castle as this might have been his choice of residence.

Vampire

His gray eyes burned with an incandescence, and the long white hands that hung by his sides were not those of a human being. I think I knew everything in that instant, and all that he told me was only aftermath. What I mean is, the moment I saw him, saw his extraordinary aura and knew him to be no creature I'd ever known, I was reduced to nothing. That ego which could not accept the presence of an extraordinary human being in its midst was crushed. All my conceptions, even my guilt and wish to die, seemed utterly unimportant. I completely forgot myself! . . . I forgot myself totally. And in the same instant knew totally the meaning of possibility. From then on I experienced only increasing wonder. As he talked to me and told me of what I might become, of what his life had been and stood to be, my past shrank to embers.

It is said that many of the remaining castles in England were abandoned because of local vampire activity during the early middle ages. The one on these pages would seem appropriate for continued vampire occupation.

Here again we note that the first step into the vampire's domain is through a hypnotic fascination, mainly produced by the promise of eternal life quite outside human values and duties. The longing for oblivion, away from mundane preoccupations, pleasures, and obligations, must surely be the door through which the vampire is invited into the potential victim's life; to take it, annihilate it, and transform it into something supernatural, into a strange sort of existence that runs parallel to human life and yet is irredeemably separate from it, since it feeds on it as its main purpose. In a sense, therefore, the wish for eternal life endowed with superhuman power becomes the greatest sin of the ego. And vampirism then, the punishment of such sin.

As Louis, the vampire and his initiator Lestat, kill their first victim, Louis becomes aware of why fate chose him for the transformation into a supernatural being,

I had seen my becoming a vampire in two lights: the first light was simply enchantment; Lestat had overwhelmed me on my deathbed. But the other light was my wish for self-destruction. My desire to be thoroughly damned. This was the open door through which Lestat had come on both the first and second occasions. Now I was not only destroying myself, but someone else.

Louis, who still retains some human feelings, wishes to die, for he finds this new form of existence unbearable and abominable. Lestat then attacks him to complete the ritual transformation of a human into a vampire. Louis remembers that the movements of his lips raised the hair all over his body, sending shocks of sensation to every part that was not "unlike the pleasure of passion." Louis is blocked to paralysis while Lestat sucks his blood. Then something extraordinary happens to complete the ritual, for Lestat bites his own wrist and gives it to Louis to drink from, for him to savor a vampire's pleasure for the first time.

I drank, sucking the blood out of the holes, experiencing for the first time since infancy the special pleasure of sucking nourishment, the body focused with the mind upon one vital source.

Louis then hears a powerful sound, a roar at first and then something that sounds like the pounding of an enormous drum, as if a great creature approached him in a dark and alien forest. And then he hears the pounding of another drum, and the sound of both drums grows louder and louder until it seems to fill his whole body and his senses too. His temples beat at the rhythm of this powerful sound. When Lestat eventually tears his arm free from Louis's bite, the latter realizes that the sound of drums beating was in fact the sound of both their hearts, and that the partaking of each other's blood was a penetration to the very core of the other.

After this powerful experience, Louis has trespassed the threshold from humanity into the supernatural world and starts seeing the world around him through the eyes of mystery.

I saw as a vampire. . . . It was as if I had only just been able to see colors and shapes for the first time. I was so enthralled with the buttons on Lestat's black coat that I looked at nothing else for a long time. Then Lestat began to laugh, and I heard his laughter as I had never heard anything before. His heart I still heard like the beating of a drum, and now came this metallic laughter. It was confusing, each sound running into the next sound, like the mingling reverberations of bells, until I had learned to separate the sounds, and then they overlapped, each soft and distinct, increasing but discrete, peals of laughter.

This is the first account, in fiction, that describes in great detail the way a vampire sees and hears and feels after his transformation. It seems, from what we read, that since the vampire is dead he is also outside the time-frame that governs our own human actions, thoughts, and feelings; he is able to feel, hear, and sense every event, every detail as detached from time and time-bound thoughts, and is therefore able to perceive reality in its uniqueness and savor it fully. It appears as though, by having trespassed the curtain of death, the vampire is endowed with a heightened sense of reality. This would make sense, for the vampire is also more "animal" than an ordinary human being; he is a predator, he must kill in order to survive, and therefore he must listen and eye everything around him keenly and attentively in order to fulfil his purpose. He has become, furthermore, a supernatural being, and as such he possesses powers that go far beyond the human capacities we rely on for survival.

It is understandably very difficult for us to grasp a thorough understanding of the world of the "undead" – we are familiar with only three dimensions (height, width, and depth), and we have no experience outside this frame. Vampires live in a world of shadows, where matter has neither substance nor importance, where time does not exist, where life is eternal, where powers, unknown and unknowable to us, govern and move in ways that are for us impossible to comprehend.

To return to our story, Louis must rid himself of all the human waste in his body, and he goes into the garden to leave behind his last vestiges of humanity:

> *When I saw the moon on the flagstones, I became so enamored with it that I must have spent an hour there. . . . As for my body, it was not yet totally converted, as soon as I became the least accustomed to the sounds and sights, it began to ache. All my human fluids were being forced out of me. I was dying as a human, yet completely alive as a vampire; and with my awakened senses, I had to preside over the death of my body with a certain discomfort and then, finally, fear.*

The Revenant

Not all vampire victims become vampires themselves. Vampires need to kill and suck blood, whether from animals or from human beings, in order to survive. The constant fresh blood supply prevents their bodies from wholly decomposing. There is a distinction, however, between a *vampire*, who has undergone a ritual of initiation into vampirism, and a *revenant* (he who returns from the grave), or undead, who is one to have been attacked by a vampire, the blood taken, but not to the point of transformation. The revenant dies either from shock or eventual loss of blood and, is interred, but his spirit appears to his kin and friends or fellow-villagers as a decomposing body, wandering around at night in search of victims. Genuine vampires and revenants share the same method of attack upon their victims; a bite usually at the neck, or in the area of the heart. A revenant transforms all his victims into other revenants – men and animals – and

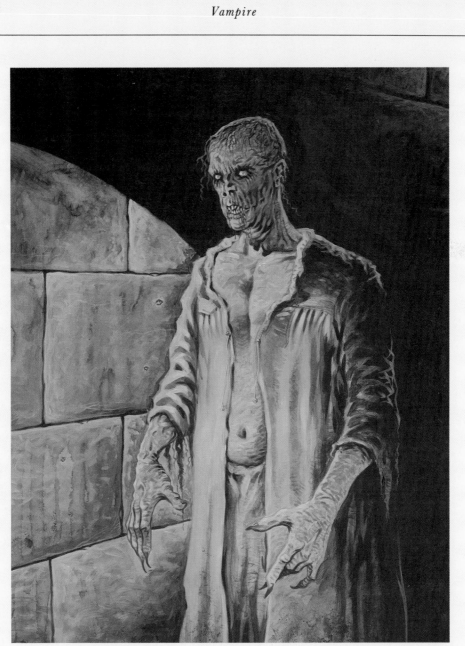

The character opposite is probably the single most unpleasant member of the vampire breed, nearer to the original concept of vampirism which was born in the hearts and fears of African tribes many thousands of years ago. The revenant was born, literally, out of the deepest and darkest realms of mankind's imagination and survives today to be reborn into the most violent movies.

———•—

when this occurs there is usually a "vampire epidemic," as slowly but surely the whole village is transformed into a community of revenants. Those who are still alive must then exhume all the bodies suspected to be undead and kill them again to end the epidemic. A vampire, however, has the choice to transform a victim into a vampire through initiation in a process of transformation carefully described in Anne Rice's book *Interview with the Vampire*.

> *The victim is never bled to the point of death, is nurtured with great care, is helped to develop the vampire senses until all perception vibrates with high sensitivity, is taught to kill, to search for a coffin, to travel with one across the world without raising suspicion, is taught how to live a wealthy life in the manner of a grand lord or lady. The process of transforming a victim into a vampire can only be described in human terms as a kind of "falling in love."*

A vampire leads thus a very different life from a revenant. The sophistication acquired in the transformation permits him to frequent high society circles and his skills at killing, without being caught, allow him to live for centuries undisturbed. A revenant has a much harder life, since he lacks sophistication and kills anyone and anything, in the open. A revenant is more likely to be caught and killed again than is a vampire.

The revenant's appearance is also quite different from that of the vampire. The vampire has undergone a process of transformation, the putrefaction of the body has been stopped and he or she tends to look intact, however pale and old he may appear. When the vampire is killed his body returns to the natural state of decomposition immediately after the stake enters his heart. A revenant, on the other hand, has no means to prevent his body from decomposing after death, and therefore he looks far more monstrous and repelling.

Trespassing The Gates of Death

asciate ogni speranza, voi, ch'entrate!" (Dante, *Inferno*)
(Abandon hope all ye who enter here).
Unfortunately, for the benefit of our gathering of precise evidence, we must now take a closer look at a rather unpleasant feature of vampirism – that of the clinical death of the human body. What exactly do we mean by human death?

If we treat an ordinary dead body – should we ever have occasion to do so – in the same way as we would treat the body of a vampire, there would be a very difference response.

In order to illustrate this rather gruesome statement we must start by examining the physical transformation that takes place after death. Apologies for the essentially graphic and often unpleasant content of this part of the book, but it has to be allowed that when we dig deep into the basic nature of vampirism, for all its superficial charm and elegance, it is still associated only with one feature of life – death.

Opposite is a gothic window at Castle Bernard in County Cork, Southern Ireland. Photographed in the Simon Marsden style, this image looks more like the gateway to hell.

The blood, after death, gravitates into the capillaries of the dependent parts, to impart a pinkish-purple discoloration to the skin, called "hypostasis". If the body is laid supine, the back of the body becomes discolored. It does not appear in those parts of the body in actual contact with the surface upon which the body rests, for example upon the back of the shoulders, the buttocks, and the back of the calves. The weight of the body is sufficient to close the capillaries in these areas and prevent them from filling with blood.

If the body has been lying face downwards, hypostasis affects the front of the body, or, in bodies which are suspended, as in hanging, hypostasis first appears in the lower limbs.

Hypostasis becomes apparent about half an hour after death, but it is not complete until some six or eight hours have elapsed. During this time it is possible to change its distribution by altering the position of the body, but, thereafter, the discoloration is usually permanent because the blood has coagulated. Although pink at first, the color rapidly darkens. When fully developed, hypostasis is dark purple in color due to the fact that the blood is no longer oxygenated.

When the oxygen in the blood is used up and, as a consequence, the blood becomes darker, one would expect the corpse to become darker as well. But since circulation has ceased, the blood tends to flow, aided by the force of gravity, to the lowest part of the body. The face, then, might be pallid and "drained of blood" (a popular description of a vampire's countenance) if the body is in a supine position.

There are, however, other changes in the color of the corpse, that are caused by bacterial infection. If, for instance, putrefaction is rapid, as in the case of death brought on by a septic infection, the veins beneath the skin generally become prominent as a bluish-brown network. Changes in color can take place with the process medically known as saponification, which preserves the body: the epidermis vanishes during this process, presumably from a combination of decomposition and shedding, and the dermis becomes darkened in bodies interred in coffins, and shades of brown or black appear occasionally.

Recent use of forensic techniques has indicated that one of the most frightening phenomena related to vampirism may have a direct scientific or rather biological reason. For hundreds of years grave diggers, exhumers and those working in morgues or hospitals have reported corpses suddenly sitting up some time after death, the body rising elegantly and without hesitation to a sitting position! Not unnaturally such events have caused considerable distress and reports have even been made of witnesses dying from shock or heart attacks as a result.

Until recently such occurrences were very simply put down to supernatural activity, and of course vampirism was a popular solution to the phenomenon, particularly as in a number of cases the bodies actually appeared to slide off the table before collapsing once more.

Within the throat and trachea regions of the body there are certain chemicals and fluids that continue to function after death. The body has its own post-death system which continues to work, preparing the corpse for its deterioration and decomposition. Among these fluids there are some that, after the rest of the fluids have dried up, contract at a later point, drawing the other organs into this "dance" of contraction. In effect, the muscles and tissues within the stomach and lower digestive tracts are reduced and in this process the body arches forwards into the sitting position.

If the arms are in a state of rigor mortis at the front of the body placed across the thighs, as is often the case, they will appear to move upwards as pushed by the lifting of the trunk, thus performing in the all-time fashion of the horror movie.

To "cut" a rather long and disturbing story short, we can sum up the general conditions of the deceased body as follows –

This listing comes from Glaister and Rentoul's dissertation on the subject and provides external, distinct signs of decomposition:

* Greenish coloration over the right ileac fossa (depression at lowest part of small intestine).
* Extension of greenish color over the whole abdomen, and other parts of the body.
* Discoloration and swelling of the face.
* Swelling and discoloration of the scrotum, or of the vulva.
* Distention of the abdomen with gases.
* Brownish coloration of the surface veins, giving an arborescent pattern on the skin.
* Development of blisters, of varying sizes, on the surfaces.
* Bursting of blisters, and denudation of large irregular surfaces due to the shedding of the epidermis.
* Escape of blood-stained fluid from the mouth and nostrils.
* Liquefaction of the eyeballs.
* Increasing discoloration of the body generally, and greater and progressive abdominal distention.
* Presence of maggots.
* Shedding of the nails and loosening of the hair.
* Facial features unrecognizable.
* Conversion of tissues into a semi-liquid mass.
* Bursting open of the abdominal and thoracic cavities.
* Progressive dissolution of the body.

Decomposition is aided by the presence of air, moisture, microorganisms, moderate temperature, and by the presence of insects. The body, however, can be

preserved in a number of ways, one of which is burial, intentional or accidental, in lime. When a body is buried in lime, decomposition is retarded and the tissues maintain their suppleness. If we were to put a stick into the hand of such a corpse, it would not be unusual for the dead hand to go on grasping, appearing not to be willing to let go. The reason for this is that the dehydrated hand remains in whatever position it was placed. And it is evidence such as this that may have frightened exhumers into believing that they were indeed dealing with the body of a vampire, at which point they might well have attempted to "kill" it again.

When a body that fails to decompose comes to the attention of the populace, then the fact is bound to cause a stir. Historically, we can count two likely explanations given by both Church and populace of this phenomenon: either the body has been reanimated by some extra-human power, a power that acts out of darkness, or the body was the dwelling place of a saint and so was immune to decay. If it was decided that the body was in fact that of a vampire, then it would certainly have to undergo the stake-through-heart process.

However, if we refer back to the bodies exhumed by the German officials in the previous chapter, we note an inconsistency. On the one hand they describe the bodies as not being decomposed, but if we apply the medical meter of judgment, given above, we can safely state that those bodies were in fact decomposing. In some instances it is noted that the superficial skin had fallen away and that a new, fresher one showed underneath. This could well be the epidermis peeling away and the dermis showing, a clear sign of putrefaction according to Glaister and Rentoul. The dermis is not a "new" skin, it simply looks raw and possibly redder in color than the epidermis that covers our bodies in life.

———— ◆ ◆ ————

On the previous page we find a grotesque nightmare entering in through our bedroom window. This image results from the fantasies fed to the Victorian virgin, who had to remain chaste for fear of ghastly reprisals.

In Greece, for instance, the swelling of the body is taken as an "unmistakable" sign of the presence of a vrykolakas (Greek for vampire). The Serbian gypsies believed firmly that if a corpse bloated before burial, then it would probably become a vampire. Bloating and swelling are viewed as prognostic of the condition of vampirism in the popular mind. Doctors, on the other hand, state that the gases produced within the intestines bloat the body considerably after death. The microorganisms that are formed during decomposition produce gas, mostly methane, throughout the tissues, and since this gas lacks an escape route it collects both in the tissues and cavities. This also explains the "wild signs," namely the erections with which the vampires seem to present themselves while lying in the grave.

The emission of blood, or blood-stained fluid, from the mouth and nostrils is also medically explained as the progressive disintegration and putrefaction of the body. The blood coagulates after death, but, depending on how death occurred, it either remains coagulated or it liquefies again. This might explain the fact that when the exhumers drove a stake through the heart of the vampire "fresh blood issued." Presumably, the common understanding at the time was that blood always coagulated after death, and if it remained liquid then this was another unmistakable sign of vampirism.

This inconsistency gives us, in fact, an important clue in relation to the making of a myth that haunts the primordial part of our minds, "the vampire has a body, and it is his own body. He is neither dead nor alive; but living in death.." as Montague Summers, a great expert in vampires and in the occult, stated. The outward signs of decomposition in the bodies of vampires are proof of the fact that they are dead; their spirit, however, is still alive, for at night it haunts houses and kills people.

This discovery helps to explain another popular belief on the subject of vampires, namely that when they were alive, they were damned, tired of living, and wishing for nothing but death. The "undead" may have been on some occasions victims of misfortune: they may have been murdered, struck by lightning, drowned, or they may have committed suicide. It is these forms of death that brand an individual as one likely to become a vampire, as opposed those who die peacefully in bed. The former unfortunates might also often have been left undiscovered for long enough to develop into monsters, growing in size, changing in color, shedding their skin. If we imagine that these events occurred mostly in rural areas, where communities were held together in small villages, defending themselves against any "evil" believed to be lurking in the vast forests that surrounded them, then it is easy to see how something unusual, such as an individual dying on his own outside the village periphery, must have struck a chord of fear and sent the mind spinning into imagined horrors. The very fact that death was considered primarily as violent and caused by unusual circumstances, was taken as a "sign:" these people were being punished for their sins on earth. The changes in the dead body would certainly have appeared repulsive and thus were a confirmation that these beings had *lost their human form* and had transformed into something else . . . into a vampire.

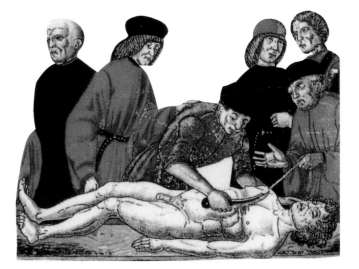

Compulsive fear, or even hysterical terror in the case of vampires, can go in sinister form hand in hand with the causes for misfortune. There are no limits in the fearful mind as to what is considered suspicious behavior for a corpse! The gypsies, for instance state that, "If, after a period of time, the body remains uncorrupt, exactly as it was buried, or if it appears to be swollen and black in color, having undergone some dreadful change in appearance, suspicions of vampirism are confirmed." Note carefully what is being said in this statement: if the body remains as it was, then it is a vampire, whereas if it changes, then it is also a vampire. The fear of vampires was so great in eastern Europe, that the living communities thought that the best way of recognizing a vampire was to list all possible anomalies in a corpse: whether it decomposed or not – the only two options a dead body has – it could still be a vampire. The fear was in fact so great that it escapes any logic we might want to find in the meter of judgment used to detect vampirism.

Admitting that there were certainly frequent cases in ancient times of "mistaken identity" when it came to vampire detection, we can now conclude, on the basis of the above evidence, that a vampire's body was in fact dead in the manner the vampire Louis explained to the young journalist in Anne Rice's book *Interview with the Vampire*.

We can also see that any deceased body can show the "unmistakable" signs of vampirism, and especially so those corpses that have remained undiscovered until the process of putrefaction is well under way.

Opposite – Bela Lugosi in the 1931 movie version of "Dracula", evoking the baroque vampire style given birth by John Polidori a hundred years before.

As in all legends rooted in ancient reportings, our case is hard to prove one way or the other, and the case is still further complicated by the likelihood of mistakes made in the past through lack of precise medical knowledge. We have now seen both sides of the doubter's coin – the mystical and the scientific, so what is the real distinction between an ordinary corpse and a vampire?

The suspicion that a vampire was at work arose only because of his nightly "doings" – if other people were dying fast and for unexplained causes, then it is reasonable to assume that *someone* must be killing them. If no one died and no other distressing events were noticed, then the deceased, however monstrous and repulsive he may have appeared, would presumably not be dug up from his grave.

So to take our investigation a step further and attempt to answer the question of how and in what form a vampire goes on living after death, we must abandon the physical world of death, whose evidence we have at this point exhausted, and enter the veiled world that lies beyond the grave . . .

Supernature

here have been a number of theories with which scholars have attempted to explain vampires, but these seem as curious as the illogical signs of vampirism we have already examined; moreover, these theories have remained just that – theories. They seem plausible as long as they are not examined too closely, for when we apply the evidence we possess, they tend to fail hopelessly.

According to one prominent theory, vampires were not dead, but merely in a coma and when they "came to life" after being discovered, they frightened people to such an extent that they were then killed properly. This theory fails because, as we have already seen, the vampires are in a state of decomposition which follows a total death. In any event, some vampires spent months, if not years, in the grave and it is highly unlikely that they were suffering during sometimes as long as a century from a chronic form of coma.

Another, more modern, explanation is given by Karl Meuli who states that "the quality of our thinking makes it impossible for us to bring about the conception of our non-existence." The villager, terrorized by an epidemic of vampires, was not, however, contemplating his own death, but that of others, and Meuli skirts around this problem by stating that we cannot conceive the death of anyone else either.

We must seek elsewhere for our answer, in a domain that is no longer human.

Many witness reports indicate that a vampire cannot be actually caught, nor killed while it is walking around, since it is a spirit. The only way of bringing death to the vampire is in the grave, when the spirit has returned to its original abode.

There is a widespread belief that vampires are born with two spirits, one of which is dedicated to the destruction of humankind. In the past, people believed that the spirit resided within the heart, so that when killing the evil spirit of the vampire a stake must be driven through the heart, the heart cut out, burned, and the ashes scattered in flowing water. It was also stated that one could recognize that a vampire has two spirits by the fact that it often talks to itself.

Occultists testify that there exists enough evidence to prove that spirits who are unable to find peace after death come back to reside in a living human body, and in so doing annihilate the individual's spirit and take over that body. These evil spirits seek revenge, for they have either died prematurely and are not willing to abandon the earthly life, or they are completing an unresolved task in this world, often an evil one.

There is also the belief within the occult world that the spirit can not only travel and reside in any body of its choice, but that it may take a number of guises. The spirit may, for example, become invisible, or take a white, incorporeal form, or a form similar to the body it inhabits. It can be a breath, a shadow, a light or torch (birthday candles are the modern remnant of this belief). It can be a white dove, or even a bee. If the spirit belongs to an evil person, then it can take the form of a small black dog.

Primitive cultures believe that the spirit is casually attached to its body, for it is reasoned that during sleep, unconsciousness, and in death, it leaves the body entirely. The physical changes that the body undergoes during sleep – the slowing down of the pulse and breath – are attributed to the spirit leaving the body. Among the numerous reasons attributed to the dead body's ability to live on is the fact that their image, or spirit, can appear in other people's dreams after they have died. It is considered unwise to wake someone up suddenly, for he or she may be dreaming and the spirit may not have the chance to return to the body, in which case the person will die. In the eyewitness accounts examined earlier, we saw that many of the victims were visited by the vampire in sleep; the dreams of choking and blood-sucking were in fact visitations from the "undead."

> *"Now I lay me down to sleep,*
> *I pray the Lord my soul to keep;*
> *If I should die before I wake,*
> *I pray the Lord my soul to take."*

This prayer has been taught to children worldwide for many centuries; its original meaning (traced back to the twelfth century) was certainly connected to the fear of the soul's propensity to be stolen by evil influence.

The combination of gravestone and holy cross took many forms. The cross in the foreground was in fact originally intended to represent the penis as a glorification of fertility and to help encourage the earth to bring good harvests. Its presence as a totem to death is therefore perhaps ill-conceived.

Mirror Images

Since the soul travels, there are a number of circumstances in which it can remain trapped while out of the body. The popular belief that it is bad luck to break a mirror originates in the idea that mirrors contain the spirit in the form of a reflection. Throughout many parts of Europe the custom of turning mirrors towards the wall when a member of the household dies is still prevalent. The spirit is thus prevented from reflecting itself and returning to reanimate the body. If a mirror is placed before a vampire there is no reflection, as the spirit is wandering and never present in the body. Our reflection occurs then, not in our physical but in our ethereal presence.

In some areas of central and eastern Europe it is considered important to pour out all standing water from containers after a death has occurred, as water can function like a mirror and reflect the soul's image. In Romania all containers of water are covered at night because it is believed that the spirit, while wandering during sleep, might fall into water and drown. The people of Macedonia take the opposite view and leave a container full of water beside the grave to ensure a bad spirit, if it has remained within the grave, be entrapped should it decide to leave the deceased to torment others at night. In European folk customs we find the practice of pouring water between the corpse and the location where the person died, to provide a barrier between the dead and the living and to prevent the spirit from returning to life. All these customs relate in some way to the original belief that vampires and water don't mix well – that if a vampire crosses water, the evil spirit will remain trapped in it.

We must remember that most of these customs were developed in pre-industrial Europe, when mirrors were not only scarcely available, but of low-quality so that the reflection was distorted and probably no better than in water – ever changing.

Just as mirrors are covered when death occurs and water is used to prevent the spirit from molesting the living, the eyes too are believed to reflect images and thus to capture stray souls. It is therefore extremely important to avoid the gaze of a dead man, for death is reflected in his eyes and consequently into the observer's, bringing certain death. And here is the origin of the vampire's hypnotic stare – reflecting death upon the victim and thereby hypnotizing him – enticing him into the vampire's world, literally staring the victim to death. In funerary practice we still observe the practice of closing the eyes of the deceased. Our modern interpretation of this ritual is to give sleep to the dead, but the original purpose was to avoid the reflection of death upon the living.

Many cultures believe that "the other world" is quite literally a mirror reflection of this world. Everything is upside-down by comparison with this world. The spirit world is reached by movements contrary to the normal: in fact, devil worshipers read the Lord's Prayer backwards as part of their Black Mass.

What is good here, is evil there. Matter corresponds to shadow, life to death, high to low, and so on. Souls of the "other world" seek to come back and take possession of a dead body in order to go on living.

Often, the spirit leaves the body at the point of death but decides to come back, reanimating the body to create a vampire. For this primitive and long established reason, the living will take steps to ensure that the spirit is successful in leaving the body: doors and windows are opened, the house is swept clean, the dust and dirt put outside to ensure against the possibility that the soul is hidden in a corner somewhere.

Hidden Practices

f we examine funereal practices carefully, we can see that the rites of transition and of incorporation of the deceased into the world of the dead are not only elaborate and complex but very often hide meanings that we have either long forgotten or found alternative, more rational reasons for. They have been developed over the centuries to ensure that the spirit completes its journey safely to the "other side," that it rests in peace there forever, and that it does not come back to take other lives with it.

We might, for example, consider the function of mourning in a different light: it is normally seen as an expression of sorrow and respect for the deceased, but many cultures view it as a necessity, not a courtesy. The length of the mourning corresponds to the period in which the corpse is thought to be in a dangerous position, for fear of the return of the spirit. In southern Italy and Spain, women mourn ten years for their fathers and husbands and five years for their brothers and sons. Often, professional mourners are hired. The women may at times change their appearance: they no longer wear makeup, they cut their hair, and wear black clothes for the entire mourning period. The mourning clothing and change of hairstyle were originally intended to render unrecognizable those who were left behind. If the dead one returned, he or she would fail to recognize the first potential victim, the husband or wife.

These widespread beliefs and practices testify to the idea that the spirit is in fact quite separate from the body. A vampire can have one of two spirits: one which is evil and may take over from the naturally resident spirit in a living body; or one that has arisen from a body and returns there to the putrefying corpse, taking possession of it by reanimating it, and carrying on living as long as it can find enough victims to feed on.

Legend provides us with some glorious conditions for vampirism, both for the vampire's reasons for being born as such and the environments, causes, and circumstances of their birth.

Opposite – the fallen angel beside an old grave – the hungry vampire would use the graveyard as a last resort to find fresh bodies recently buried, their blood yet uncongealed, in days when the dead were thrown unceremoniously into the ground. Especially criminals, who, it was believed, did not deserve holy ritual were simply dumped into open holes, very often at crossroads where the devil would take their souls.

Disposed To Be a Vampire

hose that are different from the normal, those that are unpopular, or great sinners, form the most likely candidates either to be taken by vampires or to come back from the dead. In eastern Europe, for instance, alcoholics are believed to be prime candidates for vampirism, and in Russia people were exhumed just because they were alcoholics while living.

Those who commit suicide are firmly believed always to come back from the dead and claim new lives. In the past, they were refused burial in the churchyard and nowadays suicide is still considered a crime.

Christians who convert to Islam are believed, in some countries, to become vampires, as are priests who say Mass in a state of mortal sin, as well as children whose godfathers stumbled upon reciting the Apostles' Creed at their baptism.

In general, witches, sorcerers, the godless, the evil-doers, werewolves, robbers, arsonists, prostitutes, deceitful and treacherous barmaids, and other different and dishonorable people have the potential to come back from the dead and take the guise of a vampire.

The gravestone was placed above the head of the body in the grave so that, if a returning spirit should occupy the dead, the body would not be able to sit up. Only criminals, alcoholics and great sinners were not accorded formal burial, just the sorts of character one might expect to be occupied by floating souls!

Where there was no gravestone, a vampire could come to life again.

Where there was moral weakness, therefore, life could be forever.

Destined To Be Vampire

ery often people become vampires through no fault of their own. Among them are those that were conceived during a holy period according to the Church calendar, and the illegitimate offspring of illegitimate parents.

Potential vampires can also be recognized at birth, usually by some abnormality, as when a child is born with teeth, with an extra nipple, with a lack of cartilage in the nose (remember the fallen nose in one of the vampire accounts), with a split lower lip; or with features that are viewed as bestial, such as fur down the front or back, or a tail-like extension of the spine, especially if it is covered with hair. If a child is born with a red caul, or amniotic fluid, then it is regarded in many parts of Europe as predestined to become a vampire. The caul is, under normal circumstances, white. If it is red it must be dried up, stored and crumbled into the child's food after a fixed period of time in order to prevent vampirism.

Interestingly, much of the judgment applied to these first two sections of vampire "qualifications" is reminiscent of the Eastern beliefs in karma. In the East, particularly in India, the life of an individual, if it be considered badly managed through crime or misdeeds, may dictate the quality of the next life. An alcoholic may be forced to deal with his indulgence in his next life, likewise a criminal. The tradition that believes in the chance of a soul returning to a second life, this time of vampirism and thus punishment of the worst kind, has a similar basis.

Made To Be A Vampire

he vampire does not always suck blood from the victim's neck; it may attack the thorax, the left breast, the area of the heart, or the left nipple.

In China and throughout the Slavic countries it is believed that a dead body may become a vampire if an animal such as a dog or cat, or anything animate, including even a man or woman, jumps over it. If a bat, in particular, flies over a body then there is no escape from vampirism.

If an individual's shadow is stolen, then he will become a vampire for sure – the theft, according to the most common legend, tends to occur in or close to buildings, where the shadow is measured against a wall and then secured by driving a nail through its head.

If the deceased cannot be buried, either because Mother Earth will not accept the burial, like with evil-doers who are believed to be unwanted by the earth, or because the authorities would object, then it is more than likely that the poor victim will return as a vampire.

Vampire's Undoing

There are, of course, many failures that will lead to the birth of a vampire. Not surprisingly, one example is carelessness in the carrying out of funereal rites.

It is considered dangerous for a corpse to be left unattended. If the body is buried without a priest, then it is likely to come back.

Lack of burial is the surest sign that the deceased will become a vampire.

Chapter 3

The Ways of the Vampire

Progress Towards Immortality

The vampire has traditionally led a somewhat withdrawn, perhaps even quiet, uncomplicated life. Once he has completed the process of transformation and perhaps lived some years in poorer circumstances while building up his skills and connections, his next task is likely to be to acquire a castle in some remote area, or a grand residence suitable both to secure his coffins and his victims in locations unlikely to attract attention. He is also concerned to prevent the local populace from suspecting the nature of his ways, and, at least in the past, a lord was more privy than a commoner, especially in the remote districts of eastern Europe.

He enjoys generally a parasitic relationship with those who live in the local area, as it becomes occasionally necessary for him to draw upon human flesh in the district for his continued pleasure and survival. This is a potentially dangerous aspect of his local reputation, for although he does not wish to be thought greedy and therefore dangerous to the maintenance of local population figures, he does want to maintain a certain aura of mystery and doubt among his neighbors as a deliberate policy – keeping them thus in a kind of subdued state of fear for their welfare. This gives him freedom to feed off the occasional virgin, young man, or other juicy morsel. In many eastern European districts the very name of the castle, when uttered by a visitor, may send the neighbors into a state of uncertainty, though concerted action on the part of the local population is unlikely due to a general apathy, some will say brought about by a hypnotic cloud cast by the Lord vampire.

Intrinsic Perils

he lifestyle of the vampire could perhaps be described as ascetic. In order to maintain his aura of mystery, as we have seen, he lives on the borders of society, maintaining a low profile and so has very little contact with others of his kind, except those that he keeps entrapped for his pleasure.

He is often an intellectual. His extremely long life, after all, permits him a considerable knowledge of the world around him, of culture, literature, art, and even music, though doubtless his taste in these facets of life will be suitably dark in character, perhaps covering his walls with Giotto rather than Michelangelo.

He functions in the local ecosystem for hundreds, or even thousands, of years carefully maintaining the fine balance between his need for fresh blood and the local supply. He is often a great expert in local heritage and the history of local feuds and mysterious deaths, since he has likely perpetrated a good many of the deaths himself. He will astound visitors with the extent of his detailed knowledge of events, for indeed he enjoys the mimicry of the human ego greatly and probably excels at the majority of human gifts.

———◆———

Opposite – a representation of the horrors of hell and damnation derived from the dark rituals of witchcraft. Vampirism and witchcraft almost always went hand in hand in medieval Europe. The dark forces of the devil took many forms but they were all born out of the fear of death and damnation. The witch and the vampire often were wed.

There are a few problems, however, that the vampire must face if he wants to live like a man, rather than wander in woods and deserted places. First of all he does not eat at all, nor does he exist in public during the day. Servants who have suspected their masters of vampiric practices, have revealed sightings through key-holes of charade-like dinners with empty plates, the lifting of an empty glass to dry lips and the pretense of cutting food by the scratching of the plate with unblemished silver.

The vampire must also pretend to an innumerable number of sicknesses and indispositions that prevent him from seeing people during the day. Why pretend, one may ask, if one is endowed with richness and eternal life? But the vampire is frequently made scapegoat for otherwise inexplicable phenomena. Not only are mysterious deaths attributed to him, but also floods, famines, harvest failures, and any variation of what is normal life, otherwise unexplained. The following verse, drawn from Galician folklore, testifies to the all-embracing power of the vampire:

> *The power of the vampire is very great*
> *and many-sided, even in his lifetime*
> *can kill people and even eat them alive;*
> *can bring into being, or remove, various*
> *sicknesses and epidemics, storms, rain,*
> *hail, and such; he casts spells on the cows*
> *and their milk, the crops and the*
> *husbandry generally; he knows all secrets*
> *and the future, etc. Besides this he can*
> *make himself invisible or transform*
> *himself into various objects, especially*
> *into animal forms.*

These lines illustrate the flexibility of ancient legend – the writer attempts to document the powers and doings of the vampire, ending the sentences with "etc" and "and such," thus providing sufficient poetic license to those that will follow to extend them as needed.

A Vampire's Convenience

The seclusion of his daytime rest is, of course, of the utmost importance. The coffin requires a hiding place of absolute security, for generally he is most vulnerable while within it. This aspect of the vampire's "life" reminds us that he is most at home in death and yet still, as are all the dead, most prone to danger. The coffin itself will perhaps be lined with fine silk, but must always have a layer of soil from the native grave in which the vampire was interred at his death. The trappings of his death process are always required and the original earth is a part of this – the earth to which he should have gone – dust to dust, ashes to ashes – almost as though he inevitably accepts that final destruction must come.

The servant most readily available to a vampire – the master – is likely to be a revenant the vampire maintains at a perfect balance between life and death, maintaining trust by service and in return being helped against ultimate decay, for without the vampire's attention the revenant would certainly deteriorate as we have described before.

This servant pledges his will to his lord and acts as if he were perpetually hypnotized – keeping curious visitors, such as students of the occult or inquiring doctors, at bay and providing a constant supply of rats and other small animals for fresh blood, barring all doors and access to the master's place of rest, and making sure that when away from home, the conditions necessary to the life of his master are maintained. This servant has probably the only close relationship with the vampire, for he is permitted to witness the whole truth of his master's life. Otherwise the vampire is a lonely creature who must live in isolation, kill and drink blood, commit horrendous acts of inhuman behavior, and yet still possess human feelings. He will never, over centuries, come in contact with other creatures with whom he might share thoughts, feelings, sensations. Two vampires could never live together, for their need to kill would soon exhaust the local supply of fresh blood, and their unparalleled lust for human life's fluid would bring them constantly in conflict with one another.

The Bloodlust of the Countess Bathory

erhaps one of the most famous cases of the vampire's lust for blood and power was that of the Countess Erzsebet Bathory of Hungary, whose life has been portrayed in many stories and even on film. She is said to have drunk and bathed in the blood of six hundred and fifty young virgins in the belief that the practice would rejuvenate her. Victims were recruited, with the help of her subordinates, on the pretense of recruiting servant girls at the Castle Csejthe, her home. All of them, inevitably, fell prey to her insatiable lust for blood. In the winter of 1610, however, the castle was raided after an intended victim had escaped and warned the authorities of the crimes committed by the Countess. Blood-drained bodies were discovered, some pierced with tiny holes all over the flesh; some girls were found alive, but partially drained and one was found completely "emptied" of blood, but still warm. Her accomplices were tried and beheaded, and the Countess was walled up in her own bedroom and fed through a small hole until she expired in 1640. It is still not known whether the Countess was a true vampire or simply an insane woman with a particular passion for youth. There are those in the area of her original home who say she still walks and still kills.

Today, of course, it is becoming increasingly difficult for a vampire to find a remote area with a castle where he can live peacefully and enjoy a local community of villagers to supply him with the fresh blood he needs for sustenance.

Driven by hunger, vampires have been known to sweep cities and outlying suburbs in search of victims. In 1980 the *Weekly World News*, an American newspaper, revealed in its 2nd of December issue under the heading "Vampire Killings Sweep the U.S." the following:

> *A terrifying wave of vampire killings is sweeping the nation, and experts believe that the bloodthirsty murderers may be responsible for as many as 6,000 deaths a year.*
>
> *Police are investigating dozens of eerie murders which have left pale, broken*

bodies of victims drained of blood — sometimes horribly mutilated and bearing the evidence of ghoulish Satanic rituals.

They include:

A double murder in New York City in which the victims were so completely drained of blood that the medical examiner could not get enough for a blood sample.

Six Sacramento, California people who were murdered by a man who later admitted drinking the blood of his victims.

A 7-year-old Bronx, N.Y. boy who was found hanging upside down, the blood drained from his horribly mutilated body.

Nine hobos who were killed in California, each on the night of the full moon, by a murderer who also drank their blood.

"There is no doubt that these creatures need as much human blood as a pint a day," said Dr. Stephen Kaplan, Chief of the Vampire Research Center in Elmhurst, N.Y. "They can't buy it. It requires a prescription. I believe that these people sometimes grab hitchhikers to satisfy their blood lust."

We cannot be sure, of course, that this is the work of vampires or revenants at all, but simply some crazed human being. Nevertheless, there are sufficient reports of this nature across the world each year for us to believe that at least some of them are the work of authentic vampirism. The legend is kept very much alive in the late twentieth century.

Dressing for Dinner

A vampire can live for hundreds, or even thousands, of years. During this time he is able to collect considerable wealth and a proper status amid the more obscure titlings of noble families. As he undertakes to live the life of a lord, he must dress accordingly. In order to circumnavigate the problem of being indisposed during the day, and therefore unable to visit the local stores – hatters and tailors – the vampire will, instead, richly reward those who open the doors of their stores after dark, as well as those who are prepared to meet in elegant restaurants in the small hours of the night to conduct economic transactions. The illustrations on these pages might well be the modern equivalent of the best dressed vampire, one that we might not even recognize as a vampire, except on closer examination.

The traditional vampire dresses as a gentleman. The most common attire, familiar to all, is the long black cape that, when opened, resembles the shape of the wings of a vampire bat. (Incidentally, vampire bats were named after vampires, not vice versa – the story that a vampire will become a bat at night is untrue.) The material of the cape is of a satiny, shiny, slippery silk, and no investigation has yet been able to identify exactly its quality and origin. Some say it is woven by the vampire himself after final discovery of his transformation – the secret being handed down from vampire to vampire, never to be revealed to mortal humans.

The vampire can envelope his entire body and head within the folds of the cape, slightly raising his arms above the head in a pose which has become familiar to most of us. In so doing he creates, for the human onlooker, a "black hole" making

himself literally invisible. In this guise he can hide anywhere, or leave altogether unseen.

Beneath the cape the vampire wears an elegant black tuxedo, with long tails that reach to below his knees. His sharply pressed trousers are of course also black.

The tuxedo is invariably worn with an evening shirt and a stiff collar spotlessly white, the collar noticeably higher than normal in order to disguise the deathly pallor of his face. The vampire will never show himself in full light, but chooses only candlelit rooms, the fashion of his garments camouflaging his true appearance.

The tuxedo, trousers, and evening shirt are also fashioned from the same sleek material as the cape in order to facilitate swift movements. He is also aided by the fact that he lives outside human time, and his bodily movements are therefore extremely rapid, so fast, in fact, that they become almost imperceptible to the human eye.

To accompany the elegant garments, he will wear patent leather shoes, polished to perfection by his hypnotized attendant.

As a modern diversion from tradition, we have, on these pages, added some more extravagant fashion to the vampire's wardrobe. The modern vampire, after all, with so many centuries of learning, permits himself the indulgence as well as the camouflage of twentieth-century disguise.

Here comes that dark, shadowy figure once again, lurking in the places we would be ill-advised to venture. In this case Bela Lugosi as Dracula.

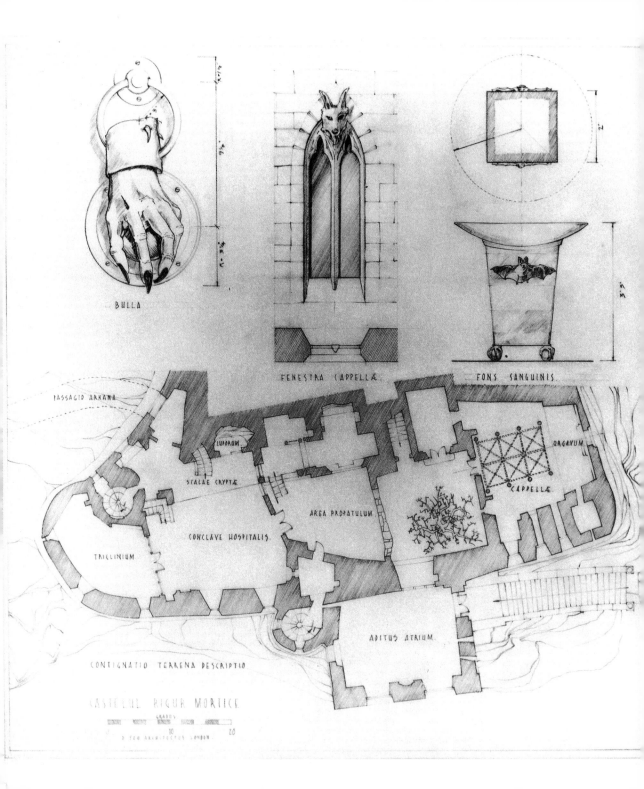

BULLA

FENESTRA CAPPELLÆ

FONS SANGUINIS

PASSAGIO ARKANA

LUPORUM

SCALAE CRYPTÆ

TRICLINIUM

CONCLAVE HOSPITALIS

AREA PROPATULUM

QAGANUM

CAPPELLÆ

ADITUS ATRIUM

CONTIGNATIO TERRENA DESCRIPTIO

CASTELUL RIGUR MORTICE

GRADUS

10   20

D FEO ARCHITECTUS LONDON

ALTITUDO

In the plot of Bram Stoker's novel *Dracula*, there is talk of building a special home for the count in Europe. We are left in doubt as to whether he completed this project, but if he had, the architectural plans might have looked something like this.

CASTELUL RIGUR MORTICE

GRADUS

0   10   20

D.YEO ARCHITECTUS LONDON.

Chapter 4
In Search of Count Dracula

The most famous fictional portrait of the aristocratic vampire is found in the novel *Dracula* by Bram Stoker. Stoker was the first to bestow this musical-sounding name to the monster, and Dracula was, thereafter, to be immortalized in numerous feature films and fictional stories as the archetypal vampire: aristocratic, disturbingly ugly, always pale and gaunt, an emaciated creature with pointed ears and long fingernails, dressed in a black cape and tuxedo, one who entices his victims by hypnotizing them with his stare and whispering softly in that thick Hungarian accent.

Dracula was for a long time thought to be a product of the wild imagination of Bram Stoker. However, the outstanding and extremely detailed geographical, historical, topographic, and folkloric context in which the novel is set leads us to believe that Stoker may have undertaken the journey from London to "Dracula country" himself, or may have done extensive research on eastern Europe and Romania before writing the work.

Count Dracula is based on the character and deeds of a legendary Romanian prince, known to historians as Vlad Dracul the Impaler, whose fame as a ruthless, clever, and bloodthirsty prince and leader of armies trespassed the borders of Romania and reached central Europe and even England, Stoker's native soil.

Vlad Dracul lived in a rural region of Romania called Transylvania, and ever since the publication and success of Stoker's novel the area has been identified as "Dracula country." Many a vampire hunter, as well as students of the occult, medical doctors, and simply curious tourists have undertaken the journey to research and discover a glimpse of the famous Count, to study his ways and habits, or, more sadly, to put an end to his murderous existence, since, with the passing of time, Vlad Dracul came to be identified with his fictional reflection, Dracula the Vampire.

A Journey Into Dracula Country

o embark upon the vampire trail is to undertake a journey of mystery and danger that leads us to a country that looks and feels like those lands we dream of in fairy tales: great expanses of dark and thick forest, across the Carpathian mountains, and into the misty and remote valleys of Transylvania on the hills of which stands Dracula's castle, eerie with the memories written on its walls of past impalements, torture, and cruel and bloody deeds.

We provide here a guide for the journeyer, warning him and her that this should on no account be treated like a "holiday" for it will open doors to matters that mankind has never seen or lived through before.

From New York or London, or indeed, any other city in the world, the first stop must be Munich, that beautiful city in Bavaria, Germany. On arrival in Munich the best hotel to stay at is the Hotel of the Four Seasons (Vierjahrzeiten Hotel): Jonathan Harker, the main character in Bram Stoker's novel, stayed there, as did all the other explorers and vampire hunters of history. The hotel is one of the main stepping stones in the vampire trail: its glorious rooms invite one to collect one's thoughts and to prepare for the adventure into the wilderness.

From Munich we climb aboard the express train to Austria's capital city – Vienna. The journey takes us through some of Europe's most startling and beautiful country, and from Vienna we continue on to Budapest, in Hungary. Vienna and Budapest sit on opposite banks of the Danube and the train journey follows the large and slow curves of this great flowing river. The magnificent city of Budapest is the gateway to eastern Europe, the new and more open world following the recent fall of communist suppression. It is also the last post of central Europe, and from here on the traveler enters the real eastern borders of the continent, quickly becoming enveloped in an atmosphere of romance and mystery, for this part of Europe is truly and recognizably different from any other, drawing the traveler back into a time when vampires really did have sway over the villages and people. Primitive, basic times filled with high winds and strong fears which still live in these often bleak lands.

TRANSYLVANIA

WALLACHIA

BULGARIA

NIKOPOLI

Zamosnivar
Gyalu
Clausenburg
Zaz Regen
Maros Vasarhely
Bistritza
Piatra
Roman
Skinti
Todoresti
Ountzriesti
Kirlizi
Podesti
Vasloui
Hus
Lipovtz
Sermieni
Tokstiki
Elizabethstadt
Segesvar
Medgyes
Gimes Pass
M. Tar
Bakou
Kalimanesti
Toupelatz
Karlsburg
Okna
Trotus
Chakani
Birlat
Kir
Mondriska
Balonesti
Hermanstadt
Alouta R.
M. Mogoura
Vazarhely
Foldvar
Kronstadt
Adioude
Inkoresti
Pancha
Beresten
Zeresti
Poutzeni
Tekouch
Peki
Boitza Mines
Rothenturm Pass
Bouza M.
Betzen
Bouska
Ungouren
Milkov R.
Fokchani
Uncheny
Gighitza
Galar
Martinest
Vezir Kioi
Brailo
Livadzel
Volkan
Draganest
Ronkow
M. Bilka
Kimpolung
Kimpina
Valeni
Plopeni
Rimnik
Kulniou
Bouzeo R.
Gradijest
Osman Agha
Outaro
Simbotin
Kosta
Salatruk
Kurte D'Argish
Rimnik
Munikhest
Branest
Tishuna
Tirgoctul
Bour kesti
Babeni
Dregojest
Pitesti
Milojest
Krikoven
Tergovist
Ploiesti
Klimasou R.
Berleshta
Matiarasa
Souponest
Vetritz
Vultarest
Bareny
Thebest
Gaiesti
Jalonitza
Lipoven
Matamouk
Marsineni
Orach
Malatzan
Aminoasa
Voitest
Obtaschy
Marciesen
Skif
R. Neazen
Khenderlita
Orsicheni
Krounz
Maltezi
Strebaja
Zinzeren
Motru
Slatina
Marschinelu
Burgareny
Argish
BUKHOREST
Khotina
Jalonitza
Slobodzi
Zlota
Borogan
Futesti
Jablonitza
Batzkovo
Mirila
Gretschi
Cholonesti
Arambatz
Babile
Kopaseni
Kurtesti
Obiliesti
Kalarach Marsh
Pisjulgardokilos
Krajova
Sirjan
Brehkoveni
Hipotest
Lada
Vadulat
Koman
Oltenitza
Warestu
Tatar
Silistria
Kusinurul
Kortateli
Radova
Kurakal
Draganest
Rusvede or Kuchi
Mogura
Odivoja
Kapouka
Kalipetra
Kutchuk Gainar
Kusjgur
Modavitz
Kalefat
Skrupetz
Rotunda
Branistia
Wadastra
Moldoven
Nagovan
Wogatza
Vede R.
Puchintzi
Tija
Ghiurgevo
Orjova
Maratin
Bo Jestaw
Rustchuk
Tzarnawoda
Siniuki
Armanlik
Buiuk Guinar
Jenikioi
Demir kioi
Slakte
Lom
Zibrulanka
Vizderina
Janova
Turna
Zimmin
Bizonzi
Sarineba
Turkchili
Aidoglu
Mellxolvatz
Poinhar
Plewna
Hutalitch
Bela
Gabova
Torlak
Rasgrad
Kulujeh
Erekli
Kosliska
Kuli
Poinia
Komeno poli
Janitza
Isker R.
Karadji
Nikup
Eski Djuma
Osman Bazar
Jenibazar
Tubi
Dewnal
Ala
Butandik
Bergofcha
Sirisjnik
Vratza
Chirikova
Loftcheh
Agatovo
Iswor
Arapli
Selvi
Turnova
Slataritza
Eski Stambol
Dibula
Pravadi
Dubrewtzi
Brusin
Telovo
Lupenina
Starekli
Bebiova
Maras
Boghaz Pass
Djenjeh
Keuprik

From Budapest the journey continues to Cluj in Romania, approximately six hours by train to the largest city of Transylvania. In Stoker's novel, Cluj is named "Klausenburgh," the Anglicized German spelling of the name, since in his time this area was within the jurisdiction of the Habsburg Empire. Jonathan Harker, the hero of Stoker's novel, stayed at the Hotel Royal, today called the Continental.

Cluj represents the heart of Transylvania, a city of extremely ancient ethnic mixes of population: the Saxons in the south, the Wallachians (or Romanians), the Magyars (or Hungarians) in the west, and the Szekelys in the east and north, who claim to be descended from Attila and the Huns. The name Romania originates in the ethnic origin of its population, for this area was the easternmost province of the Roman Empire. The native language of the Roman soldiers stationed there was Latin, and the Romanians take pride in their Latin roots, a unique heritage in eastern Europe, where the spoken tongues are largely Slavonic. The Romanians are strangely cautious, shy people who have very largely retained their gentle peasant ways, particularly in the countryside. The recently ended dictatorship under the dreaded Ceausescu family has left its mark on the land and the people, holding them almost as though in a frozen state of development. Ceausescu himself was thought perhaps to have been a vampire, perhaps, according to the continued stories of outlying areas, still walking the nights in search of victims. In any event the atmosphere of Romania satisfies the vampire hunter's desire of uncertainty and adventure – the glorious scenic value of the land somehow undercut with shadow.

After a good night's rest, the traveler will take heart in tasting the local *mamaliga*: "a sort of porridge of maize flour" which remains the national and very nutrient dish of the Romanian peasant. For his lunch in Cluj, Jonathan Harker partook of paprika chicken and "umplutura," an eggplant dish. These three dishes are so much part of the culinary fare of Transylvania that it is said that even Count Dracula offers them to his guests, while he remains seated in the inimitable stillness of the meditating vampire without tasting anything, of course, for his diet is somewhat restricted.

From Cluj it is possible to enter Dracula country only by car. The journey to Bistrita is about day long. The surrounding area is largely forests of oak, beech,

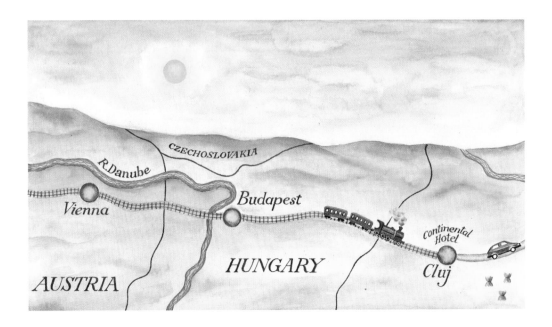

and pine. Gentle streams break the greenness of the valleys and altogether the view is so pleasing to the eye that it is hard to imagine how movie makers depicted it as a sinister, bleak, primeval, and dangerous landscape. Every now and then, one can see a castle or a hill-fort perched on top of a steep hill. Haystacks are neatly piled by the landworkers on the edge of the cultivated fields, and the farms can be identified by their fuming chimneys in midafternoon, when the work is finished and the men and women return home for a cup of warm soup after their hard day.

The people of Transylvania are both deeply religious and superstitious: by the side of the road the traveler will notice many crosses to protect the road and the fields on the side, but also to bless and protect the worker and journeyer.

Students of folklore will assert that superstitions abound in this northern part of the country, where the local villagers still believe that the forces of good and evil are constantly fighting for supremacy, taking in their stride human destiny and action. There is little science here to break the pattern of mystery.

The peasants believe, for instance, in *nosferatu*, or *necuratul*, which literally means the "unclean one" and in Romanian applies to the devil. The *Ordog* – in Hungarian meaning Satan – is believed to roam around the dark forests at night. It would be inadvisable to utter the word *strigoiaca* – meaning female vampire in Romanian – for it is believed that, being more mischievous than her male counterpart, she will appear as soon as she is summoned and take a life with her. The word "vampire" derives from the Slavic *vampyr*, and for sure this creature is well known to the Romanian peasant. The villagers have recourse to the powers of the church (holy water, the cross, and prayers), as well as herbs such as garlic, wolfbane, and petals of wild roses that are locally grown to combat their fears and to send away the evil creatures when they appear. There is nothing in this that the Romanian farmer would laugh at, for the conditioning of history is too long and unbroken to be termed superstition. It is only we in the West who term it so, degrading its value. One visit to this extraordinary country is enough to convince anyone that there are more things in heaven and earth than we could possibly be aware of in our restricted western philosophy. For this is the land of the vampire first and before all else.

Bistrita is located in the extreme east of the country and near the border with Moldavia and the Soviet Union, amid the Carpathian mountains. From Bistrita we can proceed across the pass of Prundul-Bargaului. The description of the area in Bram Stoker's novel is still accurate today.

> *Before us lay a green sloping land full of forests and woods, with here and there steep hills, crowned with clumps of trees or with farmhouses, the blank gable end to the road. There was everywhere a bewildering mass of fruit blossom – apple, plum, pear, cherry; and as we drove by I could see the green grass under the trees spangled with the fallen petals.*

The ultimate and living Prince Dracul was truly the real thing. His escapades around the beleaguered kingdoms of eastern Europe were echoed by the sounds of dreadful torture and slaughter.

Home of the Blood Drinker

*I*t is at Borgo Pass (the Anglicized version of Prundul-Bargaului) that the traveler finally reaches Dracula's castle.

...a vast ruined castle, from whose tall black windows came no ray of light, and whose broken battlements showed a jagged line against the moonlit sky.

It is here that the Count, "a tall, old man, clean shaven save for a long white mustache" lives. He is clad in black from head to foot, possibly in the fashion of a local nobleman of the time. He states,

Here I am noble; I am boyar; the common people know me, and I am master.

The word *boyar*, a Slavic word, means a member of the land-owning nobility in the Romanian language.

We do not know, truly, whether Dracula still lives in Romania. The fictional character in Stoker's book, was clearly based on the real life Vlad Dracul, a man of immense capability, power, and violence who is documented to have remained alive for more than two hundred years. In Bram Stoker's story Van Helsing, the vampire-hunter who courageously follows John Harker's footsteps from London to Bistrita to find and kill Dracula, gains knowledge of the vampire from his friend "Arminius of Buda-Pesth." Arminius Vambery was also a real man, a notable scholar and orientalist, and a contemporary of Bram Stoker, who often traveled from Budapest to London and deposited his studies on vampirism at the British Museum, at that time the largest library and source of knowledge in the world. Arminius Vambery seems to have discovered a rare document in which Count Dracula was referred to as a "*wampyr*, which we all understand too well." The word in essence means "blood-drinker."

In the novel, Count Dracula's ancestry goes back to "wolf country." The Dacians, Romanian ancestors, often described themselves as "wolf-men," and their

Once again we find representations of death etched forever – as though the sculptor wished to remind us of our deepest fears.

banner was the head of a wolf with the body of a snake.

Count Dracula is described by Van Helsing as possessing a "mighty brain, and to be an erudite of new tongues, politics, law, finance, science, and even of the occult," all attributes that the Count shares with his historical alter-ego, Vlad Dracul.

Was Vlad Dracul the first well-known vampire in history, on whose character, lifestyle, and deeds the legends were molded and grown? Or is Count Dracula the still-living Vlad Drakul, surviving as a vampire for hundreds of years, and silently domiciled in Romania?

Prince Dracula the Impaler

racula gained fame far beyond his position in world politics, greater even than his time in history, a rough and dangerous period beset by constant war, almost as dreadful as our own. He was infamous in Romania and its neighboring countries during his lifetime for committing the worst crimes history had known of; worse, some say, than the crimes committed by Caligula in Rome. He created a "forest of the impaled" which lined the roads to welcome invading troops and indeed all visitors at the borders of his country. Pregnant women, children, young and old men were staked, the sharp poles thrust between their buttocks, the body being pulled downwards until the sharp point appeared through the throat or top of the head, the wooden pole was then planted in the monstrous forest. This was the first sign to deter anyone, intended to prevent crime

◆

Streets in the villages of Transylvania today still resemble those of the distant past, with only the overhead telephone wires indicating to us that modern technology has occurred. The people still suffer from the same fears.

or treason against the terrible Drakul leader of this wretched country. When emissaries refused, out of custom, to remove their hats in his presence, he told them that he wished only to honor and strengthen their custom, and nailed the hats to their heads, a cruelty that Ivan the Terrible of Russia was later to adopt.

After Drakul's apparent death, his cruel charisma was heard of across the lands on the tongues of monks traveling from Romania to the German and Austrian provinces. Military leaders emulated some of his war techniques, hoping to follow also his success in fighting back the Turkish armies who, throughout his reign, constantly threatened invasion of his country. His bloodthirsty nature became the subject of the first horror stories ever to be published in fifteenth-century central Europe, and the reading offered such wicked pleasure to the public that these early books became international bestsellers at the time, selling nearly as many copies as the Bible.

Whether a heroic leader of armies or a monster, Dracula seems to be still more interesting than his fictional romantic counterpart, and thanks to extensive research carried out by vampire hunters and other scholars interested in the subject, he can now be revealed in full light within the historical context of his ravaged times.

Opposite – the original palace of Vlad Drakul in Tirgoviste, Romania – the place where this awesome and violent Prince tortured and commanded, murdered and terrified his people, and whose legend gave life and death to Bram Stoker's story of Count Dracula in the nineteenth century. The palace still stands, as a proud reminder of a violent and effective ruler.

The Dracula Clan

Prince Dracula, who ruled the territories that in modern times constitute Romania, was born in 1431. Europe, which extended at the time from the Atlantic Ocean to the Black Sea and the Baltic coast, represented much more than a united civilization. Powerful dynastic ties of vassalage and honor linked countries together, and, even though the Renaissance had made its mark upon European culture, the Church still had an all-pervasive authority and the strata of society were still locked in the tight grip of the feudal structure.

Dracula's birthplace, Transylvania, is the region that was inhabited from ancient times by the Daco-Romans, or, as they came to be called in more modern times, Romanians. Having been conquered by Rome in AD 101 and AD 105, the Dacians, the original dwellers, gave up the struggle, and the area was incorporated within the Roman Empire and witnessed massive immigrations from all corners of the Empire. The region is located beyond the Carpathian mountains and was described by early chroniclers who traveled there as "trans-silva" which in Latin means literally "over-forest". The Carpathian mountains are densely forested and the name gives an exact visual description of the region.

Because of its geographical position, in very close proximity to the Black Sea and the territories of the Ottoman Turks on the southeast and of the Tatar's Golden Horde on the northeast, Transylvania and the whole region, known today as Romania, was very vulnerable to invasion by the infidels, who, by conquering these territories, had then free access to central Europe. Romania was somewhat similar to regions in the Middle East today, a flashpoint of political turmoil.

Turkish invasions meant widespread destruction, burning of villages and fields, and the killing of large proportions of the population. But the Turks not only brought death in the form of war, they also brought such terrible diseases as syphilis, tuberculosis, leprosy, and smallpox. These ravagings, together with natural calamities such as floods, bitter harvests, earthquakes, and swarms of locusts imported from the East, compelled the remote peoples of the country into a state of total loss of innocence and a great reliance on what we now call superstition, firmly believing in the power of evil, which had to be combated with the consultation of oracles and soothsayers. Travelers to eastern Europe at the time noticed a marked belief in "false" idols, the burning of witches and all other kinds of superstitious behavior.

This then is the climate that forms the cultural cradle to the young Vlad Dracul, the true-life founder of the Prince of Darkness. But be careful not to judge (in the same way as perhaps Victorian or even more modern travelers have done), that historical background, for as we have seen a great many of the traditions and legends of these people were grounded in a very practical requirement – the presence of mystery as a force towards understanding. Evil was as solid a presence in their lives as the land, the harvest, and the clothes they wore. It arrived on their doorsteps in the form of constant war, poverty, and struggle, and the witches' or shamanic magic they believed in was a very real form of understanding, working in not dissimilar ways to our modern scientific values.

Among Vlad's ancestors, Mircea the Great, Dracula's great-grandfather, became famous in history for his diplomatic skills and for successfully conquering new territories. His main seat of power was Wallachia, a region bordering with Transylvania. In order to avoid submission to the Turks, Mircea the Great signed a treaty of alliance with Sigismund of Luxembourg in 1395. After the treaty, Mircea took part in a crusade led by Sigismund against the Ottomans.

———— • ————

On the previous page – Vlad Drakul's statue in Tirgoviste, Romania, the face giving an accurate rendering of this awesome man.

Opposite – a graveyard overlooking Sigishora, Vlad Drakul's birthplace in Romania. A dark and disturbing place.

It was customary at the time to send sons of noble families to be trained and instructed by other nobility for a number of years, and, usually, the two families had vested interests or were linked by a tie of vassalage. Because of Mircea's relationship with Sigismund, Vlad, his grandson and next in the line of succession, was sent at an early age to his court. Vlad, as the heir to the throne of Wallachia, sought the protection of Sigismund in the defense against the Turks. Sigismund thus inducted Vlad in the Order of the Dragon, which granted him the grace of the Prince. The Order was founded by the Holy Roman Emperor in 1387 with the character of a secret fraternal society. Like many other religious orders of knights, its objectives and duties were to protect the German king and his family, to defend the empire, to propagate Catholicism, to protect children and widows, and, of course, to fight the infidel Turks. The reason for the secrecy of the Order seems to have been the undeclared ultimate aim to gain political supremacy in Europe for the House of Luxembourg.

In February 1431 Vlad was made a knight of the Order of the Dragon. Among the rules of the Order there were those that give us some interesting clues into the making of Dracula's legend. The following was required from a new knight: the wearing of two capes – one green – reminiscent of the dragon's color, to be worn over red garments representing the blood of the martyrs. The other cape was black, later adopted by Bram Stoker's Count Dracula, to be worn only on Fridays or on the occasion of a celebration. In addition, each member of the Order was required to wear a medallion with the insignia of the dragon artfully created by a master craftsman. The dragon was represented with two wings and four paws out-

---

Opposite – the watchtower of Vlad Drakul's palace in Tirgoviste, Romania, from where the dreaded Prince watched his subjects impaled and tortured in the courtyard. What souls still wander hereabouts, still remembering the horrors of their lives?

Wie facht sich an gar ein grausſen
liche erſch:ockenliche hyſtorien von dem wilden wütrich.
Dracole wayde. Wie er die leüt geſpiſt hat. vnd gepraten.
vnd mit den haüßtern, yn einem keſſel geſoten. vñ wie er die
leüt geſchunden hat vñ zerhacken laſſen als ein kraut. Itz
er hat auch den mütern ire kind gepraté vnd ſy habés müſ
ſen ſelber eſſen. Vnd vil andere erſchrockenliche ding die in
diſſem Tractat geſchriben ſtend. Vnd in welchem land er
geregiret hat.

stretched, jaws half open, and its tail curled around its head and its back cleft in two, hanging prostrate in front of a double cross. This symbolized the victory of Christ over the forces of darkness. The medallion had to be worn at all times until the member's death and it was to be placed in the coffin after death.

When Vlad returned to his native country, he was called "Dracul" by the landowning nobility, the boyars of Wallachia, since they recognized his honor as a Draconist, or member of the Order of the Dragon (draco in Latin). However, the people of Wallachia at large, unfamiliar with Vlad's knighthood, seeing a dragon on his shield and later also on his coins, called him "Dracul" with the meaning of the "devil," because in orthodox iconography – particularly those icons depicting St. George slaying the dragon – the dragon represented the devil. The word drac, moreover, can either mean the dragon or the devil in the Romanian language. The word Dracula adopted by Bram Stoker and others was the name given to Vlad's son, since the suffix "a" means simply "son of" in Romanian. The entire family of Vlad came to be known to the populace and even in history books as "Dracul." Dracula was literally, then, the son of Dracul, or the one reborn from Dracul – as we shall see.

The bloody deeds in Dracula's career and the double meaning of his name contributed to the evil implications by which he became known. Thus a legend was born.

As soon as Vlad was made a knight of the Order of the Dragon, he swore allegiance to the Emperor and was given his official staff of office and declared Prince of Wallachia. However, Vlad's dreams of taking possession of the Wallachian throne did not materialize immediately. According to Wallachian rule, any son of the Prince, whether legitimate or not, could claim the throne as long as he was the eldest. While Vlad was away being educated at court, his half-brother, Alexandru Aldea, had seized the throne. The Emperor wished to continue his recognition of Alexandru as the Prince for political reasons and appointed Vlad, despite his new admission in the Order, as military governor of Transylvania with the task of watching the bordering area.

Vlad Dracul decided to establish his headquarters in the fortress of Sighisoara because of its central and strategic position. The hillside fort had unusually thick defensive walls of stone and brick three thousand feet long and had recently been rebuilt to withstand even the strongest artillery the Turks could muster. In addition, there were 14 battlement-capped donjons (massive inner towers), each named after the guild that bore its cost – the tailors, jewelers, furriers, butchers, goldsmiths, and so on; the massive towers made the fortress impenetrable.

The early Princes of Romania shared with the Ottomans the "harem philosophy" and made little distinction between legitimate wives and concubines, since the only thing that really mattered in the suitability for the throne was to be "of the royal male bone." However, Vlad Dracul sired three legitimate sons; the second son was also called Vlad Dracul, born in December 1431, and he was to become world famous as Prince Dracula, the Impaler.

Vlad Dracul's main aim was to gain possession of what he considered his legitimate throne in Wallachia, even though it was still being occupied by his half-brother. Finally, in 1434 Sigismund, seeing that Alexandru's relationship with the Turks was too close for his liking, ordered Vlad to form an army from Transylvanian soldiers and to take possession of Wallachia. Vlad Dracul fought the Turks and with his army, in 1436, entered Tirgoviste, the capital of Wallachia, and became Prince with the sanction of the Emperor.

For young Dracula, life at his father's new court was a wholly new experience. He was of eligible age for his apprenticeship into knighthood: he was taught swimming, fencing, jousting, archery, court etiquette, and the more refined aspects of horsemanship. He was also introduced to political science, the principles of which were in essence Machiavellian, since it was written that it was much better for a prince to be feared than to be loved; this way of thinking must have strongly molded Dracula's personality.

Previous and opposite page – Vlad Drakul's tortures and methods of execution were the most ghastly the world has ever devised.

Local tradition has it that the young Dracula was almost morbidly fascinated from a very early age by the criminals being led from jail to the Jeweler's Donjon, where they would be executed by hanging.

In 1437, however, Sigismund, King of Luxembourg and patron and protector of the Dracul family, died, leaving Wallachia and its ruling family exposed to the growing assaults and possessions of the Turks. So, shortly after Sigismund's death Vlad Dracul signed a pact of alliance with Sultan Murad II of Turkey. It seems that Vlad Dracul used to accompany Murad II on frequent raids of Transylvania, during which killing, pillaging, and burning of villages occurred, which undoubtedly built the legend of the bloodthirsty nature of the Dracula family.

After the death of his father, young Dracula was held a captive prisoner of the Turks, where he served as an officer in the army. During this time he had ample opportunity to learn all the methods of torture employed by the Turkish forces on prisoners of war. The Koran, for instance, prescribed that sexual initiation between two men should be started by the seducer wounding the would-be lover with his sword before intercourse. Impalement of prisoners seems also to have been a customary form of punishment.

Despite all the learning and experience Dracula accumulated in the Turkish army, he was still a prisoner of the Sultan and longed to seize the throne of Wallachia in much the same way as his father, Vlad Dracul, had done before him. Dracula thus decided to flee the court of the Turkish Sultan and to find refuge in Moldavia, a neighboring state of Wallachia, where he hoped to find protection and to be able to put together an army to put him on the Wallachian throne. After a few adventures and failed attempts, Dracula finally became the official prince of Wallachia in 1456, barely 25 years of age.

The beginning of his reign was hailed by the passing of a comet over Europe, and astrologers of the time generally regarded this as a celestial sign, an omen of bad luck, and a prelude to earthquakes, illnesses, plagues, wars, and other numerous catastrophes. Dracula, on the other hand, saw it as a fateful start to his dominance of Wallachia and inscribed the comet on one side of his coins, the other bearing the Wallachian eagle.

Dracula established his main residence at Tirgoviste, which was not only the seat of power, but also the center of the nation's social and cultural life. Dracula's palace, in today's standards, was of modest proportions, dominated by a watch-tower he had built from which he could survey the countryside and keep vigil for an impending attack from the Turks, and from which he could also observe the daily slaughtering he ordered in the courtyard below. The Chindia Watchtower still stands today and can be visited upon embarking on the vampire trail. Next to the winecellars, storage rooms, and the baths, there can still be seen numerous torture chambers where he kept his dying prisoners.

The boyars, the class of noble landowning families, formed, by tradition, the council of Wallachia on which even the Prince had ultimately to depend for orders and matters of administration and justice. The boyars, therefore, held even a stronger power than the ruler, and it was in their interest to elect the weakest possible prince – the one least likely to intervene in their decisions. The central power was thus unstable, and there had been a rapid succession of princes, with a rate of two years of reign per prince. Dracula was soon to change the political situation dramatically and overthrow the power of the boyars in favor of a centralized seat of power which he headed with an iron fist. Dracula also sought personal revenge, since the boyars had killed one of his brothers by burying him alive, a crime he could not forgive.

The oldest Romanian chronicle cites the events that took place in the spring of 1457,

> *He (Dracula) had found out that the boyars of Tirgoviste had buried one of his brothers alive. In order to know the truth, he searched for his brother in the grave and found him lying face downwards. So when Easter day came, while all the citizens were feasting and the young ones were dancing he surrounded them ... led them together with their wives and their children, just as they were dressed up for Easter, to Poenari (seat of the famous castle Dracula), where they were put to work until their clothes were torn and they were left naked.*

Popular tradition held that Dracula first impaled the children and the wives in the courtyard of his palace, and then the men were put to chains and led to a location known as the Source of the River, a journey that took two days. Here he ordered them to reconstruct the ancient castle which was in ruins. Dracula had given orders to the villages surrounding the castle for brick ovens to be built as well as lime kilns. The boyars, under constant threat of the whip of Dracula's guards, formed a chain from the villages where bricks were being manufactured, to the walls of the castle which they laboriously rebuilt. Local folklore claims that inside the castle there is a secret passage that leads to within the bowels of the mountains, reputedly used by Dracula for his mysterious practices. In the superstitious minds of the local peasants, the belief that a "Dracula-curse" is associated with this *evil* place is still firmly held. They say that a golden flame sometimes lights up in the sky at night, and this is taken as the ill-obtained treasure that Dracula extracted from the boyars, and no one should try to find the treasure lest he succumb to the terrible curse.

To replace the boyars, Dracula created his own nobility, much in the same fashion as the early Neapolitan mafia, formed in great part by men of plebeian origin. Breaking the tradition by which the lands and riches confiscated from a boyar were given to another nobleman from the same privileged class, Dracula gave them instead to this mass of men, who owed their power to his will entirely and had a ruthless and vested interest in the survival of his regime, one that carried out the duties alloted to them by the dreaded Vlad with the intended violence with which the Prince ordered them.

The exalted idea of his own power, however, not only drove Dracula to reduce the class of boyars to little more than obedient servants, but extended to the administration of heavy punishment to whoever dared to offend him, intentionally or not. The following is an account which has survived to our own day, of an Italian diplomatic delegation that had come to Wallachia from Genova.

> *I have found that some Italians came as ambassadors to his court. As they came to him they took off their hats and hoods facing the prince. Under the hat, each of them wore a coif or a little skullcap that he did not take off, as is the habit among Italians. Dracula then asked them for an explanation of why they had only taken their hats off, leaving their skullcaps on their heads. To which they answered, "This is our custom. We are not obliged to take our skullcaps off under any circumstances, even an audience with the sultan or the Holy Roman Emperor." Dracula then said, "In all fairness, I want to strengthen and recognize your customs." They thanked him, bowing to him; and added, "Sire we shall always serve you with your interests if you show us such goodness, and we shall praise your greatness everywhere." Then in a deliberate manner this tyrant and killer did the following: he took some big iron nails and planted them in a circle in the head of each ambassador. "Believe me," he said while his attendants nailed the skullcaps on the heads of the envoys, "this is the manner in which I will strengthen your custom."*

It is said that to see for himself how the work on the land of his peasant people was progressing, Vlad Drakul the younger roamed across the countryside in disguise, particularly at night. He wanted to know how the peasants lived, how well and how much they worked, and what they were thinking about. Sometimes he would stop at individual peasant houses and ask all manner of questions. This particular trait was to be adopted by the romantic vampire as well: he showed concern toward his villagers not because they farmed his land profitably, but rather because they represented a source of fresh blood. Both the fictional and the historical Dracula seem to share the role of monster and protector at once, gripping

the populace within a painful and unbreakable bond.

The following ballad testifies to the methods imposed by the Prince on the peasants of this beleaguered land.

One day Dracula met a peasant who was wearing too short a shirt. One could also notice his homespun peasant trousers, which were glued to his legs, and one could make out the sides of his thighs. When he saw him dressed in this manner, Dracula immediately ordered him to be brought to court. "Are you married?" he enquired. "Yes, I am, Your Highness." "Your wife is assuredly the kind who remains idle. How is it possible that your shirt does not cover the calf of your leg? She is not worthy of living in my realm. May she perish!" "Beg forgiveness, my lord, but I am satisfied with her. She never leaves home and she is honest." "You will be more satisfied with another since you are a decent and hardworking man." Two of Dracula's men had in the meantime brought the wretched woman to him, and she was immediately impaled. Then bringing another woman, he gave her away to be married to the peasant widower. Dracula, however, was careful to show the new wife what had happened to her predecessor and explain to her the reasons why she had incurred the princely wrath. Consequently, the new wife worked so hard she had no time to eat. She placed the bread on one shoulder, the salt on another, and worked in this fashion. She tried hard to give greater satisfaction to her new husband than the first wife not to incur the curse of Dracula.

Prince Dracula punished the parasites of society, the beggars and vagabonds, extremely harshly and cruelly to set an example for the rest of the population so that they may work hard and not revolt against his rule. There is one example of this, that is so well known that it has, through the centuries, been translated in several languages: German, Russian, and Romanian. In this instance, drawn from the Romanian version, Dracula purges Wallachia of the beggars, the sick, and the poor.

> *Having asked the old, the ill, the lame, the poor, the blind, and the vagabonds to a large dining hall in Tirgoviste, Dracula ordered that a feast be prepared for them. On the appointed day, Tirgoviste groaned under the heavy weight of the large number of beggars who had come. The prince's servants passed out a batch of clothes to each one, then they led the beggars to a large mansion where tables had been set. The beggars marveled at the prince's generosity, and they spoke among themselves, "Truly it is a prince's kind of grace." Then they started eating. And what do you think they saw before them: a meal such as one would find on the prince's own table, wines and all the best things to eat which weigh you down. The beggars had a feast that became legendary. They ate and drank greedily. Most of them became dead drunk. As they became unable to communicate with one another, and became incoherent, they were suddenly faced with fire and smoke on all sides. The prince had ordered his servants to set the house on fire. They rushed to the doors to get out, but the doors were locked. The fire progressed. The blaze rose high like inflamed dragons. Shouts, shrieks, and moans arose from the lips of all the poor enclosed there. But why should a fire be moved by the entreaties of men? They fell upon each other. They embraced each other. They sought help, but there was no human ear left to listen to them. They began to twist in the torments of the fire that was destroying them. The fire stifled some, the embers reduced others to ashes, the flames grilled most of them. When the fire naturally abated, there was no trace of any living soul.*

So great was the fear of impalement that throughout Dracula's reign, theft and other crimes completely disappeared. It was not so much the virtue of the Machiavellian prince, but rather his tortured mind that imposed this clean order. The memory of his cruelty remains stamped in the tales drawn from Romanian folklore.

If any wife had an affair outside of marriage, Dracula ordered her sexual organs cut. She was then skinned alive and exposed in her skinless flesh in the public square, her skin hanging separately from a pole or placed on a table in the middle of the marketplace. The same punishment was applied to maidens who did not keep their virginity, and also to unchaste widows. For lesser offenses, Dracula was known to have the nipple of a woman's breast cut off. He also had a red-hot iron stake shoved into a woman's vagina, making the instrument penetrate her entrails and emerge from her mouth. He then had the woman tied to a pole naked and left her exposed there until the flesh fell from the body, and the bones detached themselves from their sockets.

Opposite – close by Vlad Drakul's castle lie the gravestones of those he murdered and tortured, standing in rows within a dark wood, the souls perhaps still haunting one of the most terrible scenes of history.

Dracula's Death, Dracula's Birth

ittle is known of Dracul's place of burial. Ancient Romanian chronicles state that he was buried at Snagov, where an ancient monastery that Dracul had helped to rebuild while he was still alive still stands, albeit in ruins, on an island in the middle of a still lake. In the superstitious imaginations of the people of Snagov, the terrible figure of the Impaler is still thought to haunt the grounds surrounding the small and perhaps deceptively peaceful church.

Surrounding the lake on all sides is the dense forest of Vlasia. The island of Snagov commands an excellent view and is furthermore protected on all sides by water. Even in winter, it is said, when the lake is completely frozen, a cannon shot from the island could break up the ice and thus drown all the incoming enemies. A popular folklore tradition states that the monastery was rebuilt by Dracul in the form of a fortress, and that the treasures his party had stolen from the boyars were kept within the holy walls; the monks, however, fearful of tempting the Turks with the treasures, threw them into the lake where they still could be found.

Other peasant narratives tell of Dracul's crimes on the island. It is believed that he kept the monastery as a prison and that he tortured many in its cells; the recent discovery of decapitated skeletons, with the skulls placed alongside the pierced body, seems to give foundation to this legend which claims that the Prince carried out his impalements even here.

Although a series of excavations have been completed by archaeologists, no certain remains have yet been found to be those of Prince Dracul in the foundations of Snagov.

There is an ancient legend, however, that tells of the fearsome devil's school in the mountains, mentioned even by Bram Stoker in his novel, which reputedly the Draculs attended.

> *They (the Draculs) learned the secrets in the Scholomance, amongst the mountains over Lake Hermannstadt, where the devil claims the tenth scholar as his due.*

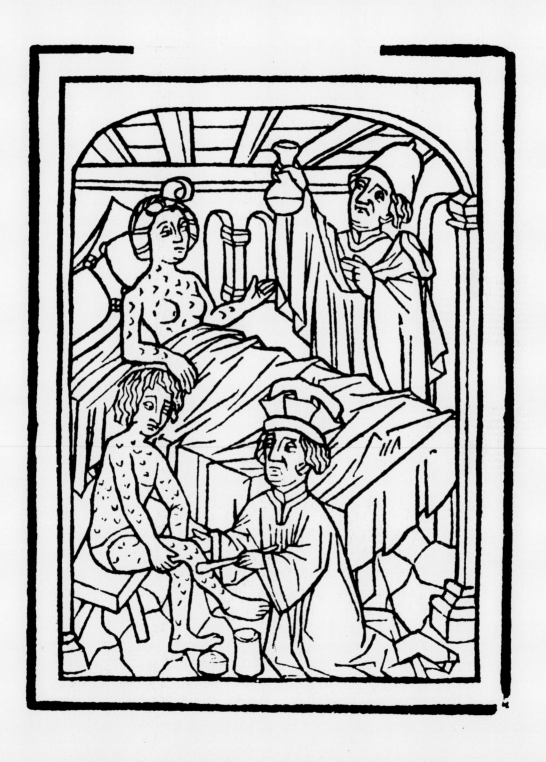

There is further evidence of the school in Western chroniclers.

> *. . . a school supposed to exist somewhere in the heart of the mountains, and where all the secrets of nature, the language of animals, and all imaginable magic spells and charms are taught by the devil in person. Only ten scholars are admitted at a time, and when the course of learning has expired and nine of them are released to return to their homes, the tenth scholar is detained by the devil as payment, and mounted upon an* **Ismeju** *(the correct Romanian spelling of the word is* **Zmeu,** *meaning dragon) he becomes henceforth the devil's aide-de-camp. . . . A small lake, immeasurably deep, lying high up among the mountains of Hermannstadt, is supposed to be the cauldron where is brewed the thunder, and in fair weather the dragon sleeps beneath the water.*

The word Scholomance derives from the Romanian Solomari, meaning the "students of alchemy." It is a corruption of the word Solomon, the wise judge in the Bible, whom legend turned into an alchemist. Since legendary places are kept secret, or their true location is hidden with the name of a different town, it may be that Dracula was buried at the secret school of Hermannstadt, or that the secret school was situated at Snagov. The monks of Snagov explain that even nowadays they start storing away food and goods in midautumn in preparation for the harsh winter that will cut them off from the world altogether for many months. Snagov, moreover, was an ancient place of learning. May it be that the imagination got the two places confused, intertwining each one of the legends to form a third which describes where Dracula was buried and explains his magical and "weird" practices? The credence that Dracul attended the Scholomance school would explain the passage from the historical to the fictional, supernatural character.

It is said that the most important day of the year for the Romanian peasant, and indeed for much of the old Germanic and eastern European people, is St. George's Day, on the 23rd of April. On the eve of St. George's Day many occult meetings take place at night in lonely caverns or within ruined walls, and where all the ceremonies usual to the celebration of a witches' Sabbath are put into practice.

WITH
MORN
THOSE
ANGEL FA

WHO

WH

This same night is the best for finding treasures. On the night of St. George's day all the treasures begin to burn, to bloom in the bosom of the earth, and the light they give forth, described as a bluish flame resembling the color of lighted spirits of wine, serves to guide mortals to their place of concealment.

It may be that on the same night a favored mortal searching for Prince Dracula might see a light come forth from the waters of the lake where his treasure is drowned . . . for the Dragon, Dracula's symbol, favors on that night all search.

But most strange of all the legends and stories surrounding Vlad Drakul is that he returned to the area two hundred years later and was seen and witnessed by many as the son of the same family, born into different times. His appearance was similar to the depictions of his dreaded great-great-great grandfather, though he was seen to be more noble and less obviously violent in his ways. The times into which he returned were more peaceful times and the new Prince Dracula fitted well. These same stories uphold that the Prince of Darkness never died and this is why his coffin has never been found – because he carries it with him even today.

If we analyze the nature and extent of the crimes committed by Prince Dracula during his reign, we might draw the conclusion that he was one of the greatest and cruelest psychopaths in history. It has been estimated that his victims range in numbers from a minimum of 40,000 to a maximum of 100,000, which is nearly a fifth of the total population of Wallachia, which at the time incorporated approximately half a million inhabitants.

But Dracula did not by any means restrict himself only to impalement. Stakes stood permanently prepared in his courtyard at Tirgoviste and in various strategic places, such as public squares and marketplaces. It is said that the stakes were carefully rounded and bathed in oil so that the entrails of the victims should not be pierced by a fatal wound immediately. Dracula was said to be often present when each leg of the victim was tied to a horse and he personally whipped both horses so that they would go running in different directions, whilst the attendants held the body and the stake firmly in place. Some impalements, however, were not from the buttocks up, but from the navel, the heart, the stomach, and the chest.

And it is this gruesome Eastern practice of driving a wooden stake through the heart or a vital part of the body, which contributed to the belief that a vampire can be killed only in this same way. Possibly even the countless deaths perpetrated by Dracula, the Prince of Darkness, are still seeking revenge and inspire, unconsciously, the vampire hunter to administer the same punishment to the members of the Dracula species. It is true that Dracula not only killed men, but also children, the elderly, and women. Such crimes are not easily forgotten.

Dracula decapitated, cut off noses, ears, sexual organs, limbs; he nailed hats to heads; he blinded, strangled, hanged, burned, boiled, skinned, roasted, hacked, and buried alive. It is suspected that he practiced cannibalism himself, eating the limbs of those he killed, and drinking their blood; it has been proven that he forced others to eat human flesh and that he used to smear prisoners' soles with salt and honey and allowed animals to lick them for an indefinite period of suffering.

In conclusion, the madness that had taken possession of Prince Dracula and drove him to commit the worst crimes history has ever heard of was exported by monks and travelers from Wallachia to central Europe; here, among a cultured and less barbaric milieu who prided itself in having attained the "renaissance" of man, but nevertheless was hungry for tales of horror of far-away places such as Wallachia, the legend of Dracula grew disproportionately. The monster of history became alive in the pages of the earliest horror stories; some of his real traits, such as the almost physical pleasure that pain and torture produced in him, the thirst for blood, and his noble origins, were kept intact and can be found, unchanged, in modern vampire stories. Other traits, such as the long canine teeth, the hypnotic stare, and his immortality, were added partly by the fervid imagination that still quivered in memory of medieval horror stories and superstitions, and partly by the evidence, which was springing up all over Europe, that blood-drinking creatures really did exist.

Moreover, Prince Dracula was not, according to all accounts, just a psychopath and a man suffering from sexual impotence who thrilled in seeing the stake being driven through the genitals of his victims; there are a few mysteries that lead the adventurous reader from the gruesome to the supernatural and these mostly curl around his death, his coffin that was never found, and a connection between his death and an ancient school of occult learning, whose existence has until now been kept secret for centuries. And it is here that we begin to see the final connection between the death of the Prince Vlad Drakul and the birth of his reborn son – The Prince of Darkness, Dracula himself.

The interior of Vlad Drakul's private chapel.

Chapter 5
Family of Vampires

True vampires long for a quiet existence, to be lived in the great halls of castles hidden amid the Carpathian mountains, or in dark and thick forests. Anonymity is the very tool of survival of a vampire, since, as soon as his or her existence is discovered, "life" is at risk. The endless, slow monotony is interrupted only by the thirst for blood which compels the creatures to look for a victim among mortals.

There are, however, a few exceptions, as in all things of nature and supernature, for some vampires gloat in the limelight and in high society – their game of hide-and-seek with victims and vampire hunters providing a pleasant diversion to their eternity. The titillation and excitement of being swifter in movement, governed by laws outside those of the human world, to possess a unique knowledge of history by its direct experience over centuries. With the endowment of hypnotic powers that paralyze victims, the power to become invisible, to be, in other words, quite different from us mortals, all this must be an amusing distraction when moving amid human circles. As the few vampires that lead this kind of existence are so different, they are bound to become the center of attention wherever they go.

Thus, a few vampires have become very famous, and the tales surrounding these precious few have been told countless times, for they always afford great pleasure. Their success is due not only to the fact that it is the story of a supernatural, monstrous, and yet fascinating creature, but also because these vampires move among an absolutely normal milieu – a contemporary setting. Evil is perhaps still more terrifying when met in a recognizable world, rather than in a remote and foreign atmosphere. Take Lord Ruthven, for example . . .

Lord Ruthven

ord Ruthven is an English vampire, living in London, the city where he was born. The winter in London is marked by various parties held by the leaders of the *bon ton* society, and Lord Ruthven, a true nobleman, is often present – more for his singularities than for his blue-blooded rank. He spends the summers abroad, preferably in Greece where there are still so many remote areas he can visit, and where he can remain alone and undisturbed.

Lord Ruthven is cool by nature and seldom displays his wit and supernatural skills. Apparently, only the laughter of the very fair attracts him. His face, although very beautiful, is always darkened by a deadly hue and never gains a warmer tint. This does not seem to put off the hunters of notoriety, who, seeing in him the incarnation of absolute aristocratic values, often seek to obtain his affection. He has, moreover, the reputation of a winning tongue, and it is perhaps for this reason that every good hostess seeks to have him on her list of guests.

It is rumored that Lord Ruthven possesses irresistible powers of seduction as well as having licentious habits which make him dangerous to beautiful hostesses. To enhance his own gratification after the seduction, Lord Ruthven requires that his companion in sin be hurled from the pinnacle of virtue to the very lowest abyss of infamy and degradation. His preference lies with inexperienced young girls of the noble classes, although he has been known to entertain the favors of mature, and even married, women. When asked what his intentions are in regard to the inexperienced girls, he answers that they are such as he supposes all would have upon such an occasion. When asked whether he would marry the girl, after having

—————•—————

Opposite – Lord Ruthven, the fictional character from John Polidori's short story, *The Vampyre*, supposedly styled around the character of Lord Byron.

taken her virtue, he answers with a cruel laughter. Women who were previously beautiful and animated have become dispirited and lifeless after a shortlived relationship with Lord Ruthven. Others have become mad with passion, and after their affair with him the only thing they wished for was death and annihilation.

Lord Ruthven's passion seems to be aroused beyond measure when he can take a girl loved by another, especially if it is a man who considers the nobleman as a friend. Lord Ruthven himself claims to have no friends, but may occasionally act as though he favors one or other of his companions – his generosity increasing if he spies a pretty, innocent girl accompanying them. If the man tries to stop him from taking possession of the girl, Lord Ruthven will attack with a strength that can best be described as superhuman force.

Many a hurt lover has attempted to murder Lord Ruthven, and some have even succeeded – or thought they had. In one instance, the servants had placed the dead body of the lord on top of a mountain, so that it might be exposed to the first cold ray of the moon that rose after his death, his fondest wish. However, when his

companion climbed the mountain the next day he found no trace of the body, nor of the clothes. The conclusion was that the servants had stolen the beautiful clothes of the nobleman and buried the corpse so that no one would find out. Lord Ruthven had in fact murdered his companion's lover, although the latter did not know of the event, as it had occurred during the night and there was yet no suspicion of vampirism. Imagine then the horror that seized him when, upon his return to London, he saw Lord Ruthven partying again amid the elegant circles of admirers, gaining the favors of his own sister, the only friend left to him. The story ends with the man being so distraught by the loss first of his beloved and second his sister that he dies of pain and madness, whilst Lord Ruthven has glutted his vampire thirst on two beautiful young women.

Varney The Vampire

arney is a lurid creature who loves to wake up beautiful young women by scratching with his fangs at the window-panes of their bedrooms while they sleep – imitating with his nails the noise of hail beating against the glass, for his preference is to attack on stormy nights.

His face is perfectly white and perfectly bloodless. His eyes look like polished tin and when he draws back his lips, fearful teeth are displayed, projecting like those of some wild animal – hideous and glaringly white and fang-like. His nails literally hang from the finger-ends, and he likes to clash them together producing a hair-raising sound that paralyzes the victim.

His awful, metallic-looking eyes are as hypnotic as those of a serpent; his strength is superhuman.

Varney enjoys most the pleasures of profaning a young woman's beautifully rounded limbs employing the hideous manliness of his own body while making a dreadful sucking noise, drinking blood from the side of the victim's neck.

After feeding, his face becomes hideously flushed with the color of fresh blood, and his eyes have a savage and remarkable luster. Whereas before they shone like metal, after the attack they are ten times brighter and flashes of light seem to dart from them. Varney can be recognized also from the dreadful howling that issues from his throat.

Opposite – James Malcolm's *Varney the Vampire*, a story of horror and nastiness published in the British "Penny Dreadfuls" of the mid-nineteenth century – weekly magazines that ran stories for as many as 800 issues, to be read by avid fans in the same way as comic books are read today.

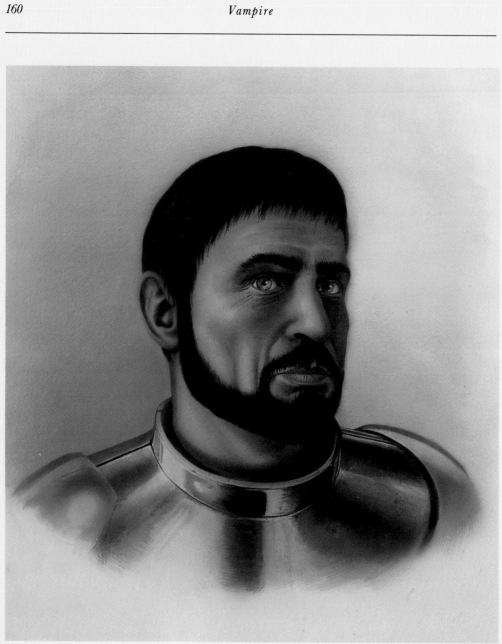

The Knight Azzo

The Knight Azzo lives at Castle Klatka, which is situated in the Carpathian Mountains, in Romania. The Castle, reputed to have been abandoned by human life but haunted for centuries, stands within the lands belonging to the Knight of Fahnenberg, the descendent of a noble Austrian family. The title of the Fahnenberg family is inherited along with the lands and possessions both in Austria and abroad. Every time the new Knight of Fahnenberg visits his castle in Romania he meets the strange and exotic Knight Azzo, who has been living there and roaming the wild surrounding forests for hundreds of years.

The Knight Azzo appears to be a man of about 40, tall and extremely thin. His features are bold and daring, although his expression is not in the least benevolent. There is great contempt and sarcasm in his cold gray eyes, and his glances are so piercing that no one can endure his stare for long. His complexion is even more peculiar than his eyes: it is neither pale nor yellow, but rather gray, like that of an Indian who has been suffering long from fever, and it is rendered even more remarkable by the blackness of his beard and short cropped hair.

He dresses in knightly clothes, but oldfashioned and neglected; there are great spots of rust on the collar and breast-plate of his armor. He carries a dagger and a sword, as do all proper knights.

Although Knight Azzo is apt to accept supper invitations from his neighbors, the Knight of Fahnenberg and his family, he never eats, claiming that his digestion is quite unused to solid food and that he lives entirely on liquids.

He likes to be addressed as Azzo von Klatka by those he entertains with his speculations on existential matters. He is drawn most readily into conversations with or in the presence of unmarried, beautiful young ladies, while he is likely to be rude, cold, sarcastic, and insulting to the chosen lady's fiance – or any young man who might dare to challenge his wit or strength.

The Knight Azzo loves everything that is peculiar and uncommon; he talks to wolves, and even these fierce beasts obey him and become like docile lambs in his presence. He claims that all things are alike; life and death, this side of the grave and the other have more resemblance, in his view, than we might otherwise imagine. He amuses himself with hunting and has been known to spend many a moonless night roaming in the dark forest and marshland surrounding Castle Klatka. He also loves to ride on a horse that never tires in the pale moonlight over hills and dales, through forests and woodlands.

The Knight does not receive or see anyone unless the moon is shining brightly. With strangers he is coldly polite and tends to speak in monosyllables. But from his way of talking, one can detect a deep hatred, a cold detestation of all mankind, with the exception of fair young ladies.

Carmilla

armilla is an anagram of the true name of Mircalla, Countess Karnstein. She has appeared, throughout the centuries, under many names, all anagrams of the original: Millarca and Carmilla are two of the most famous disguises.

The features of the Countess, however, have remained unaltered in all the centuries since her "death." She appears as a young girl, of not even 20 years of age, and of magnificent beauty. She is above the average height of women, slender, and wonderfully graceful; her movements are languid, *very* languid, and her large eyes never seem to blink and rest upon objects for long, unmoved in their gaze. Her complexion is rich and brilliant; her features small and beautifully formed; her eyes large, dark, and lustrous; and seldom has anyone seen such hair, so magnificently thick and long when it is down about her shoulders. It is exquisitely fine and soft, and in color a rich, very dark brown, with something of gold in it.

Carmilla speaks in a sweet low voice and loves to chat and entertain with harmless, sweet gossip. Her beauty, her grace, her manners, and her conversation are so exquisite that she is invited to countless balls of the noble high society.

Little is known about her, since she exercises an ever wakeful reserve towards her mother, family, origins, her life, her plans, and everything that surrounds her. She claims that her mother has extorted a promise not to reveal anything to anyone, although, in order not to hurt her friends, she constantly promises them that in good time she will tell all. She admits to only three things: first, her name is Carmilla, or any anagrammatical variation of it; second, her family is very ancient and noble; and third, her home lies in the direction of the west.

Carmilla invariably appears in the company of her mother and strikes up an acquaintance with a lovely girl of her own age, who generally lives alone with her father in some remote chateau. Young people, especially young girls, like and love on impulse, and it is endearing for their fathers to see their own daughter find such pleasure and delight in the company of such a beautiful and noble girl. Carmilla's mother, in the stories of their life together, is called away on urgent and vital

business, leaving her daughter in the hands of the fathers, who readily promise to look after her until the older Countess returns, several months later. Carmilla, according to her mother, cannot travel the far distances required, as she is in delicate health and somewhat nervous. Because of her beauty and the sincere friendship towards their daughter, the fathers always consent gladly to the Countess's will, since they can see nothing but delight and pleasure coming into their lonely homes with the presence of Carmilla to warm their hearts.

Carmilla's habits seem odd, especially so to rustic people. She does not come down from her room until very late, usually well past midafternoon. She then takes a cup of chocolate, but eats nothing. And whenever she goes out for a walk she seems, almost immediately, to feel exhausted and must either return to the castle or sit to rest on one of the garden benches. She is also in the habit of locking all the rooms of her living quarters at night, claiming that some robbers intruded in her room many years before and she has been terrified ever since of it occurring again. However, local gossip says that she has been seen wandering about in the nearby forest at night, like a soul without repose.

Carmilla loathes funeral processions, and whenever she sees one she has a fit of rage, her face turning livid, her body shaking violently, and her fists becoming tightly clenched. This, however, only lasts a few moments until she regains possession of herself and behaves as if nothing had happened.

Carmilla is a very sensuous creature; she falls utterly, desperately in love with a girl and wishes for nothing but to die with her. She kisses her cheek, draws her breath very near her neck, and holds the girl's hands tight against her own heart.

The female vampiress gained much ground during the nineteenth century – from being merely a slave of the male vampires to being a rabid killer in her own right.

This is the description of Carmilla's ardor from the hand of one of her victims:

Sometimes, after an hour of apathy, my strange and beautiful companion would take my hand and hold it with a fond pressure, renewed again and again; blushing softly, gazing in my face with languid and burning eyes, and breathing so fast that her dress rose and fell with the tumultuous respiration. It was like the ardor of a lover; it embarrassed me; it was hateful and yet overpowering; and with gloating eyes she drew me to her, and her hot lips traveled along my cheek in kisses; and she would whisper, almost in sobs, "You are mine, you shall be mine, and you and I are one forever." Then she has thrown herself back in her chair, with her small hands over her eyes, leaving me trembling.

Almost as soon as Carmilla settles in a region, there appear to be a number of medically inexplicable deaths; women who die suddenly of a 24-hour illness. At the same time, her friend and companion, Carmilla's much cherished and loved victim, receives the nightly visitations of what appears to be a large, black, and sinister cat, pacing back and forth in the bedroom with the restlessness of a caged beast. As the room grows darker and darker, the cat springs onto the bed and the victim feels a stinging pain, as if two large needles had darted, an inch or two apart, deep into her breast. Carmilla has in fact two faculties: she can transform herself into a large black cat and she can make herself invisible.

The true story of Mircalla, Countess of Karnstein is a sad and singular one. While still alive, in the year 1698, she had been attacked by a vampire and thus became one herself. An ancestor of Baron Vordenburg, the man who eventually succeeded in killing her centuries later, held the Countess as his idol and loved her greatly. Even though he suspected her of vampirism, his greatest horror was that her beautiful remains would be profaned by the outrage of a posthumous execution, as it is customary with the dead suspected of vampirism. The Baron had left a curious paper to prove that the vampire, on being killed again, is projected into a far more horrible life, an evidence which he had found in ancient books of the occult. Wishing to spare his beloved Mircalla from such a horrid fate, he journeyed to the castle of the Karnsteins and pretended to remove her remains, and changed the position of her grave, hiding it with plants so that it would remain undiscovered. Upon his death, however, he realized what he had done and left a diary in which he had made tracings and notes to guide the future vampirehunters to the spot where the grave had been placed. The diary also contained a confession of the deception that he had practiced.

———————◆———————

Castles of the early and middle ages frequently carried huge protecting statues on their tops to save the inmates from passing spirits and roving vampires and werewolves.

The village surrounding Castle Karnstein was abandoned after the death of the Countess, and the progeny of those who had served the Countess during her life of course took it for granted that she had been killed again as a vampire. Since this was a deception, the beautiful Carmilla continued to kill hundreds of women until her coffin was found, a stake driven through her heart, and her remains burned and thrown into the waters of the nearby flowing river. Nothing is known of who the distinguished lady who claimed to be Carmilla's mother might be.

Julia Stone

Julia Stone lives in a room at the top of an ancient tower which still stands in the Asdown Forest district of Sussex, in the south of England.

A portrait of her hangs in the room; it depicts an old, withered, and white-haired woman. There is an evident feebleness in her body, but a dreadful exuberance and vitality shine through the envelope of the old flesh, an exuberance which is wholly malign, and she shows a vitality which foams and froths with unimaginable evil. Evil beams from the narrow, leering eyes, and a wicked laughter comes from her demon-like mouth. The whole face has some secret and appalling mirth. The hands, clasped together on the knee, seem to shake with suppressed and nameless glee. The signature of the painting, on the bottom left-hand corner, states "Julia Stone by Julia Stone."

No one can remove the painting from the room in the tower. To begin with, it is so heavy that even three strongly built men cannot lift it off its hook. The painting, furthermore, cuts the hands and limbs of all those who attempt to remove it from its place, and, even though the cut is never visible, there is considerable bleeding. Visitors to the house, who were forced by circumstances to sleep in the room at the top of the tower, were so frightened by the portrait of Julia Stone they wished it removed despite all the difficulties.

Julia Stone is said to appear at night, dressed in some close-clinging white garment, spotted and stained with mold. She attacks her victims, usually men, by pinning them down to the bed with her superhuman strength and sucking their blood from the side of the neck. Whenever she appears there is a foul smell pervading the room, and her portrait hangs back on its hook as if it had never been removed.

The local chronicles, which can be found in the local church, tell of the attempt that was made three times, many years ago, to bury the body of a certain woman who had committed suicide. On each occasion the coffin was found in the course of a few days again protruding from the ground. After the third attempt, in order that the thing should not be talked about, the body was buried elsewhere in unconsecrated ground. The chosen ground was just outside the iron gate of the garden belonging to the house where this woman had lived. She had committed suicide in the room at the top of the tower in that house. Her name was Julia Stone.

The Girl With The Hungry Eyes

The Girl is a top model in the United States. But she is unlike any other. She is unnatural. She is morbid. And she is unholy.

The Girl is the Face, the Body, and the Look of America, but no one knows anything about her, where she came from, where she lives, what she does, who she is, or even what her name is. She has never been drawn, nor painted. All her portraits have been worked on from photographs. Neither has she been interviewed before now.

No one ever sees her, except one photographer who is making more money out of her than he ever dreamed of.

The Girl has skinny arms, a thin neck, and a slightly gaunt, almost prim face; a tumbling mass of dark hair, and, looking from under it, the hungriest eyes in the world. The reason why she is displayed all over the fashion magazine covers is for those eyes, a hunger in them that is all sex and something more than sex. Everyone has been looking for the image of the Girl: something more than sex.

The Girl has worked for only two photographers and has never given her name, telephone number, or address to anyone. She arrives for work always on time, she is never tired, and she forbids the photographers to follow her out of the studio or so much as to look for her leaving the building from the window, threatening that if they do so, they will have to hire another model.

There is a theory, conjured up by one of the photographers, that may explain the success of the Girl. Suppose the desires of millions of people focused on one telepathic person. Say a girl. Shape her in their image. Imagine her knowing the most hidden hunger of millions of men. Imagine her seeing deeper into those hungers than the people that had them, seeing the hatred and the wish for death behind the lust. Imagine her shaping herself in that complete image, keeping herself as aloof as marble. Yet imagine the hunger she might feel in answer to their hunger. This is how the Girl appears, this is what one feels when looking into those hungry eyes.

The first photographer ever to take a picture of her, and to make her famous, was the only one who eventually came to know her truth. He felt dizzy in the studio whenever she was there, attracted and strangely repelled at the same time. As the fame of the Girl began to increase, the photographer looked through all the papers in the morning to see how many of his photographs of the Girl had been published; he noticed, however, that every week there had been murders in the city which the police could find no explanation for, since the manner of killing was completely unknown.

The photographer was hypnotized by the Girl. He made a pass at her and she refused him with a smile. In the manner of men, there were many other passes, less smiles, and more refusal. He eventually decided to follow her, risking his fame in attempting to find out more about her. He saw that she waited by the side of the curb until a car, driven by a young man, picked her up. They drove off together into the night. That evening, the photographer got drunk. The morning after, he saw the face of the young man in the paper: he had been murdered.

The photographer then decided to risk it all and to walk down the stairs with the Girl on his arm after work. She asked him whether he knew what he was doing. He said he did. They went walking in the park, she was very silent and eventually sat

down on the grass, pulling him towards her. He started fumbling with her blouse, she took his hand away saying she did not want that.

What she wanted was this:

> *I want you. I want your high spots. I want everything that's made you happy and everything that's hurt you bad. I want your first girl. I want that shiny bicycle. I want that licking. I want that pinhole camera. I want your mother's death. I want the blue sky filled with stars. I want your blood on the cobblestones. I want Mildred's mouth. I want the first picture you sold. I want the lights of Chicago. I want the gin. I want Gwen's hands. I want your wanting me. I want your life. Feed me, baby, feed me.*

There are vampires and vampires, and the ones that suck blood are not the worst.

Count Dracula: Prince of Darkness

And last, but certainly not in the least, comes Dracula himself. Drawn from the ancient legends of Vlad Drakul's family, heavily embellished by the hand of Bram Stoker, we learn that the Count was a tall and visibly old man, clean-shaven except for a long white mustache – not something that is generally portrayed in the many movies – his body clad from head to foot in black without a single dash of color on any part of his body.

Stoker enhances his hero's first impression with a facility for perfect English but with a strange "intonation" and great charm. His face, on closer examination, is strong, very strong and aquiline "with high bridge of the thin nose and peculiarly arched nostrils; with lofty domed forehead, and hair growing scantily round the temples, but profusely elsewhere."

The master's eyebrows were "very massive," almost meeting across the top of his nose and his mouth, beneath the mustache, was peculiarly cruel-looking with disturbingly sharp white teeth which "naturally" protruded over his lips, these in turn showing great vitality and redness for one so evidently old. The general effect was observed to be pallor.

The combination of elegance and crudeness is brilliantly brought out by Stoker's description of Dracula's hands –

> *Hitherto I had noticed the backs of his hands as they lay on his knees in the firelight, and they had seemed rather white and fine; but seeing them now close to me, I could not but notice that they were rather coarse – broad, with squat fingers. Strange to say there were hairs in the center of the palm. The nails were long and fine, and cut to a sharp point. As the Count leaned over to me and his hands touched me, I could not repress a shudder.*

The master's breath, of course, smelled terrible, but then this would perhaps not have been so uncommon in days when cleanliness was not of the utmost importance. More significant may have been the fact that the close presence of Dracula simply caused Harker to almost faint.

Count Dracula has been rejuvenated a hundred times since Stoker wrote his most famous novel, and there are many today who would dearly love to believe that the most monstrous of vampires still walks the silent and black hills of Romania, surviving all attempts to destroy him, father of monsters, the most superb hypnotist, fabulous gentleman, and the crudest of all killers. If he does, then the world is ultimately and forever a dangerous place to be.

Chapter 6

The Vampire Library

The Horror House of Lords

In the library of any respectable vampire, many volumes may be found that exemplify a long and rich history of literature surrounding the undead. We have already had a glimpse into the darker realms of Count Dracula, Lord Ruthven, and other dangerous characters. Some of these have been given life and death only through human fantasy, while others actually lived and died in reality, such as the Countess Bathory.

The creation and continued spread of human belief in vampire legends has been fuelled most effectively by its literature, and if the vampire suffers from any form of identity crisis he or she would readily discover reassurance in the pages of books such as *The Castle of Otranto* written by Horace Walpole in 1764, which started a gothic revival in which authors professed to use all manner of devices such as drugs, heavy protein diets, and even "laughing gas" to encourage dreams of death and the dark arts to fuel their fantasies.

One of the most famous groups to bring the dark side of the imagination to the surface was Lord Byron, Mary and Percy Shelley, and Dr. Polidori , who reportedly spent many a candlelit evening in front of a large fire within a villa near Lake Geneva, concocting stories that saw publication as *Frankenstein*, by Mary Shelley and *The Vampyre* by Polidori in the early nineteenth century. The crude drug laudanum was employed to aid these bizarre imaginings, and once again, dreams were the fuel of fiction.

The most famous of them all, the Irishman Bram Stoker, had, previous to his classic study of Count Dracula, been the author of only one earlier volume, *Duties of Clerks of Petty Sessions in Ireland*, an unlikely work for the writer we associate today with the greatest vampire story in history. He suffered a terrible nightmare in 1890, while still working in Ireland as a business manager, and the bestselling *Dracula* changed his life forever. But this and the other works of the same period were far from the beginning of the world's attempts to relate the oldest legends in mankind's history.

As we will see in more detail in the next chapter on the darkest origins of the vampire, the story began even with Adam himself, whose first wife – Lilith , sucked blood and ate small children, and whose dread daughters, the Lilim, pestered priests in their dreams and generally made unpleasant nuisances of themselves.

Earliest man was accustomed to draining human blood in sacrifice to the gods and Mother Earth, who, it was believed, would not allow a good harvest if the seasonal rituals were not conscientiously performed with the slaughter of some poor innocent on the land.

The difference between the early origins which gave rise to the medieval folklore of vampirism, witnessed in earlier parts of this book, and the more modern gothic or romantic approach to the undead which appeared during the eighteenth and nineteenth centuries is the difference between the ghastly, blood-ravaging horror of true sacrifice and bloody slaughter, and a much sexier and more acceptable version which appeared later in fiction. In the original folkloric accounts, vampires, werewolves, and other horrific legendary creatures would leap on the victim, smother the face with a hairy, foul-smelling rear end, and rip the chest open to gorge like a wild animal on the twitching victim. There was nothing remotely romantic, engaging, intellectual, or even faintly human about such an attack, and the generally messy process probably took a matter of minutes before it was all over. Certainly not the stuff of bestselling novels.

———— ◆ ◆ ————

Opposite – Bela Lugosi ponders on his day-time rest place in the 1931 movie version of Dracula's story. Such a scene brings to the surface many distant archetypes.

Following the eighteenth century gothic revival, the vampire became a tall, gaunt, well-dressed figure with an extensive knowledge of worldly affairs gleaned from hundreds of years of travel and culture. He served fine wines and good food at his table (though partook of none himself), entertained his guests with intellectual repartee, and eventually seduced his female victims using a mesmeric stare, fine looks, and promises of sexual bliss. The kill was transferred from the chest cavity to the neck with implications, barely hidden, of sexual penetration and eternal servitude. The unbeatable *Interview with the Vampire* written by Anne Rice, transformed the romantic version of the vampire still further and brought it soundly into the twentieth century with wonderful flavors of passion, underworld secrets, and the deepest, darkest realms of magic.

So from the rather gross vampire monsters of writers such as Tournefort in the late seventeenth century, who fed from animals, drank huge amounts of alcohol, and stank of every unpleasant odor, we find ourselves more involved thereafter with clean-shaven, pale-faced seducers dressed in black tie and tails.

The aristocratic vampire rose to fame above his less desirable ancestors partly because of the most notorious of the nineteenth century lords – the poet Byron himself. Byron flourished both on his reputation as a writer and as a ladykiller. In fact it was rumored in the gossip columns of nineteenth century Paris and London that he had murdered his mistress and drank her blood from a cup made out of her skull.

The stories and gossip surrounding Byron were given additional strength most effectively by a series of literary and amorous events that would today happily grace the worst newspaper front covers. During a torrid and disastrous affair between Lord Byron and Lady Caroline Lamb which ended in 1815, much acrimony flew between the two participants. Lady Caroline wrote a gothic novel entitled *Glenarvon* which quite obviously parodied her ex-lover in the most scurrilous manner in the character of Clarence de Ruthven, Lord Glenarvon. The book was published in the spring of 1816.

Later that same year Polidori wrote his version of Lord Byron's feverish activities in *Vampyre*, the main character for which was named simply "Lord

Ruthven," of whom we have heard much already. Polidori evidently lifted the character for Ruthven directly out of Lady Lamb's book. But that wasn't all in this tale of complex aristocratic intrigue. Polidori's book was left unpublished during the following three years and then picked up by the same publisher as Lady Lamb's book, who published it as though it had been written by Byron himself. Lord Ruthven became a kind of vampiric Batman, appearing in various forms by various well-known authors around Europe during the rest of the nineteenth century until the concept of Byron as aristocratic vampire was almost established as a direct connection.

All this served to bring the erotic, aristocratic creature of darkness into our lives today.

Other vampires that we have seen also graced the pages of this same romantic period of literature. James Malcolm's *Varney, the Vampire*, published in 1846, was known as a "penny-dreadful" because of the cheap nature of its comic-like format. The story was issued to the public over a massive total of more than 800 pages and was subjected to much critical anxiety because of its graphic content, much of which had been lifted directly from Polidori's book *The Vampyre*. The series also derived one of its major scenes from Mary Shelley's original story of Frankenstein, where the monster leaps into Mount Vesuvius.

The group of Lord Byron, Mary Shelley, and Polidori, sitting in their villa next to Lake Geneva, was responsible, it seems, for a great deal of the output that occurred in vampire literature later that century.

But James Malcolm Rymer's book on Varney, the Vampire wasn't entirely unoriginal and formed as part of the chain of creativity that eventually helped to give life to Count Dracula himself. Within the ghastly meanderings that the story takes, there appears a certain Hungarian count who is also a vampire and the first to appear in English vampiric literature. Sir Francis Varney, the aristocratic vampire of the story was not exactly the Dracula-type but many of the characteristics of the Varney story found their way into Bram Stoker's masterpiece, mixed and matched, quite obviously from one writer to another. One of the most important aspects of this chain-reaction was the idea that a male vampire could hypnotize a female victim and then, through a mixture of sexual attraction and the exchange of blood, create a kind of tormenting love/hate relationship. We can see that this was yet another incarnation of the patriarchal social values that were so strong in the nineteenth century.

Tbe Literary Dracula

ram Stoker's sources for the writing of *Dracula* came from fact, fiction, and his dream-life. According to modern literary sleuths the fact and fiction range from such remote works of travelogue as *Untrodden Paths in Roumania*, which contains a wealth of information concerning the awesome Vlad Drakul, the Impaler, and *Midst The Wild Carpathians*, which from a fictional standpoint examines life in Hungary in the dark-light of devilish deeds. Count Azzo von Klatka, whom we have sampled briefly earlier, would perhaps have provided some of the methods whereby Dracula dealt with his unfortunate victims, and it is also said that Stoker took much from Wilkie Collins's classic novel *The Woman in White*. But Dracula was in no way simply a derivative of other creations.

Stoker's job at the time of his terrible dream in 1890 was as the business manager of the actor Henry Irving, one of the biggest stage names of the period, and in his book *Vampyres*, Christopher Frayling suggests that the theatrical behavior of the Count in Stoker's *Dracula* – swirling cloaks and loud voice – may have been the author's suggestion of his master's real-life character. This dramatic characterization was just one small part of the jigsaw puzzle that resulted in the inimitable Count. Much of the rest was drawn, as we have seen, from the ghastly "doings" of the Hungarian Prince Vlad who was a remote ancestor of Attila the Hun. But Count Dracula lived in Transylvania, not Hungary. He was a Count, not a Prince, and there could not have been the slightest chance that Dracula slaughtered his victims in quite so messy a fashion as did Vlad the Impaler.

This extraordinary combination of real and imagined horror, however, had another aspect to it, an aspect which may have arisen out of a further source. Stoker suffered from one of the most unpleasant diseases of his era – syphilis.

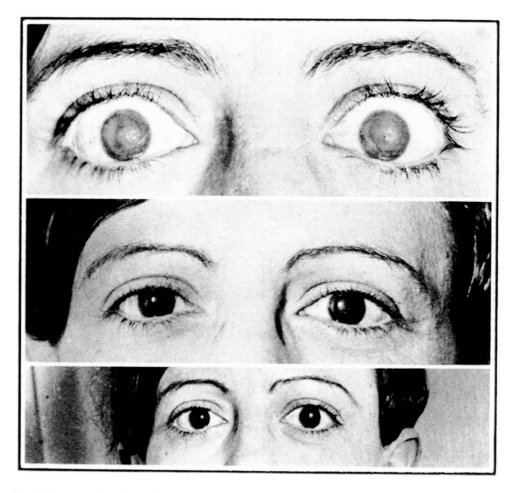

Syphilis was for the nineteenth century what AIDS is for today, or what the bubonic plague was for the Middle Ages. There was no cure, and sufferers died an unpleasant death. Stoker, while under the threat of death from tertiary syphilis, may have had access to the only known human condition which truly resembles vampirism, that of congenital syphilis.

The congenitally syphilitic child is born with certain horrific dysfunctions which are so similar to many of the most ancient descriptions of vampirism that it could well have occurred to Stoker that this was a genuine source for the "rumors" surrounding the undead.

The child may be born with all the front teeth shaped as incisors (called

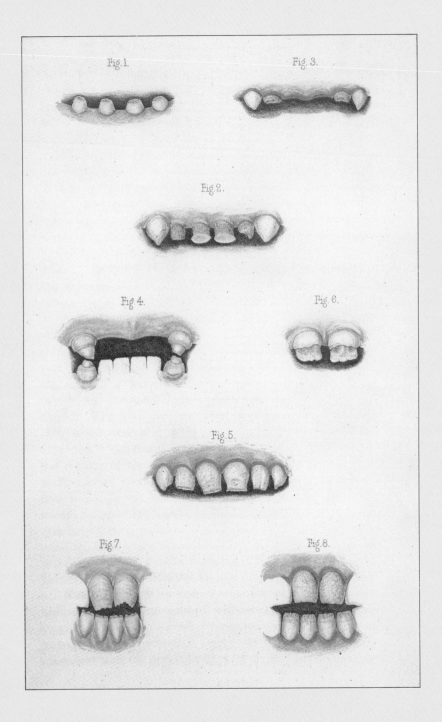

Fig. 1.

Fig. 3.

Fig. 2.

Fig 4.

Fig. 6.

Fig. 5.

Fig 7.

Fig. 8.

"Hutchkins Teeth"), sharply pointed, and ranged across the upper and lower gums exactly like those traditionally awarded to vampires. The eyes suffer from a condition which renders them pale and often encircled with a dark ring. The result is lightblindness, in other words the sufferer can see only in the dark. The palate structure is deformed so that only liquids may be ingested, and the nose bridge collapses. Babies born with congenital syphilis would also cause the mother's breast skin to rot.

Specifically, this appalling condition resembles vampirism to such an extent that it might well have formed a basis for any of the vampiric legends that have been born over the centuries. In the case of Bram Stoker's "intimate" connection with syphilis we can fairly reliably conjecture that he would have been entirely familiar with the condition.

In contrast to all this gory unpleasantness, the other most prevalent aspect of Count Dracula's character was his sexuality, for the dreaded aristocrat of the dark forest and doomy night was one of the sexiest creatures ever to grace the pages of gothic fiction. Probably the strangest set of combinations any reader could hope to find, Bram Stoker strung together a hybrid in *Dracula* that was part animal, part blue-blooded Lord, part serial killer, part genetic aberration, part immortal, and a very large part hypnotically powerful lover. Almost as though Stoker was concocting the ultimate dark-side dream, perhaps launched from the very deepest realms of his own strange life, the jigsaw puzzle of Dracula's character is brought to its final piquancy by the clear inference of sexual dominance over his unfortunate (though perhaps Stoker felt they were fortunate) victims.

Each woman that Dracula made love to, such as Lucy Westenra, became immortal, stunningly beautiful, everlastingly young, and far more attractive than ever they were before the dread vampire had performed his dastardly deed. Here again, as in everything "Victorian," Stoker makes no direct mention of the vampire having sexual intercourse with his victims, but the descriptions that enhance the sucking of blood through deep penetration of the incisors, speaks volumes of other more gentle activities happening concurrently.

Polidori's Vampyre

erhaps still more significant in some ways than Stoker's *Dracula*, was Dr. John Polidori's *Vampyre*, concerning ostensibly the terrible activities of one Lord Ruthven.

Polidori was born to an Italian immigrant family living in Central London's Soho neighborhood. His father was a literary translator of some considerable talent and fame, and son John made it early to university to study medicine. In fact, he was one of the youngest graduating students in England at the time, passing his examinations at the tender age of 19 years, in 1815. Shortly after leaving Edinburgh University he became Lord Byron's physician and suffered a tumultuous half year at the hands of the temperamental poet aristocrat, departing from his service in the summer of 1816, and returning to London to write up his experiences as a fiction in the form of the life of Lord Ruthven.

The story is clearly a version of the time he spent with Byron, with added "juice" and considerable anger, for clearly Byron was not a happy man to work with.

Polidori did not seek publication of his short work and began a novel entitled *Ernestus Berchtold* which disappeared without trace. By 1820 he was clearly suffering from the effects of severe brain damage, and in August 1821 he died at the age of 25. It was believed that he committed suicide using prussic acid, though there is some evidence that this was not the case.

This tragic, short life was not enhanced by the behavior of Lord Byron's publishers and, subsequently, Paris literary society. The short story *Vampyre* was published in 1819 under Byron's name (though Byron did not know he was supposed to have written it, even after publication), and became a massive hit in Paris.

Literary acclaim attributed the work to Lord Byron and insisted no one else could possibly have written it, ignoring Polidori completely. A full-length novel (February 1920, *Lord Ruthven ou Les Vampires* was dedicated to Lord Byron) was written as a sort of nineteenth-century "novel-after-the-movie" at the same time as no less than three stage plays: *Le Vampire* staged at the Porte-Saint-Martin theater,

Le Vampire staged at the Vaudeville theater, and *Les Trois Vampires* at the Variétés theater) based on the story of Ruthven's life, all running concurrently in the great capital city. All this, happening behind poor Polidori's back, might easily have been enough to drive him to prussic acid and an early ignoble death. His fee for writing the original story, eventually paid in retrospect by the fraudulent publishers of the work, was about 50 dollars.

Such acts of violation today would result in multi-million dollar law suits for sure.

Polidori's work may be seen as perhaps the single most significant contribution to the aristocratic, sexy, monstrous vampire cult that continued throughout the rest of the nineteenth century and still stands as a basis for romantic gothic-horror fiction today. Even the work of Anne Rice and Stephen King, our most recent horror-fiction writers, must attribute a great deal to the unfortunate Dr. Polidori.

And yet, the dread specter of death conjured up by the writers of the nineteenth century bears little or no relation to the "real" vampire. In fact, if we take a look at the earliest derivations of the word "vampire" itself, we find that its common root from most of the Mediterranean languages is formed from "vam," meaning blood, and "pyr," meaning monster, and this blood-monster was in no way either aristocratic, sexy, cultured, or immortal but simply very, very nasty.

Chapter 7

Awesome Beginnings

We saw in the last chapter how mankind has imagined his favorite vampire in recent centuries. The enduring image of the powerful, elegant and yet animal-like vampire is very much alive, but its most distant ancestors are a very different story.

> *In all the darkest pages of the malign supernatural there is no more terrible tradition than that of the Vampire, a pariah even among demons. Foul are his ravages; gruesome and seemingly barbaric are the ancient and approved methods by which folk must rid themselves of this hideous pest. Even today in certain quarters of the world, in remoter districts of Europe itself, Transylvania, Slavonia, the isles and mountains of Greece, the peasant will take the law into his own hands and utterly destroy the carrion who – as it is yet firmly believed – at night will issue from his unhallowed grave to spread the infection of vampirism throughout the countryside. Assyria knew the vampire long ago, and he lurked amid the primeval forests of Mexico before Cortes came. He is feared by the Chinese, by the Indian, and the Malay alike; whilst Arabian story tells us again and again of the ghouls who haunt ill-omened sepulchres and lonely cross-ways to attack and devour the unhappy traveler.*

This introductory paragraph begins the 1928 volume by Montague Summers entitled *The Vampire – His Kith and Kin* (published in London by Kegan Paul, Trench, Trubner and Co., Ltd) with a perfect summary of the awesome origins of the undead. So be prepared to enter now the very darkest realm of all, the most slippery, slimy, blood-ridden cul-de-sac in all of mankind's legendary corridors.

Corridors of Glower

Such of the early discussion surrounding the vampire myth was related to attempts to define exactly what they were. Definition was a matter of great importance, both in medieval Europe and during the early part of this century when Montague Summers's book was written. Both these periods were concerned with reason as a method of discounting the irrationality of the devil. In other words, if you could define something then perhaps you could control it.

The first question was, is a vampire a fallen angel? The answer came quickly that it was not, even though fallen angels could generally count among their number the intrepid "Nick;" devil incarnate, because angels were not corporeal. Vampires had solid bodies. Thus, angels were acquitted at least of this dread fate.

So perhaps the vampire is simply a demon in disguise. In order to decide on this potential inhuman "garment" for the much-despised undead, we need to ask what pertains to the demonic characteristic? Demons are known to enter living bodies and take possession of them, but demons do not have bodies of their own. They are, so to speak, post-eviction notices with a propensity to squat. But we could say this also of the vampire, for vampiric possession takes place, or so we have been led to believe, once the departing spirit of the dead has returned and taken up residence again, either in its own body or some other poor unfortunate. But there is a difference. The demon can pop in and out while the vampire is stuck inside the body it occupies. So, all ye demons may rest assured that this one awesome fate is not thine. Though it needs to be said that demons and vampires had a lot in common and could no doubt be seen of a cold dark night sniggering together along foggy country lanes, presumably comparing notes on matters of lust and horridness.

———— •••• ————

Opposite – an eerie representation of a mountain in New Mexico, to conjure up the deep dark fears of the past.

Then how about ghosts and phantoms? Is there any chance that these share the same dusty coffin as the vampire? Once again the answer is no, and for the same reason, that the ghost "ain't got no body."

The fact is, the vampire *has* a body, and it is his own body. He may even be proud of it, as was (is) Lord Ruthven. But that body is neither alive nor dead. Instead, it lives in death, almost as though the vampire has crossed over the other side and taken a body with it.

Having come to this conclusion, the early writers and "mythologers" moved along to the next step in their sometimes tortured reckonings as to the accountability of the undead state.

If death were considered by the living to be a place of rest, and it was established that vampires continued to live in death, then the fate of the vampire was definitely not pleasant. Particularly in theosophical circles of debate, the power of reason was thickly lagged with dogma and thus tended to come out both overheated and heavy on wool. You were supposed to accept that an immortal life was undesirable because the Church said so, regardless of what might really be the case. Excessive interest in sex was also considered to be bad news for the same reason, and the ability of the vampire to overpower and generally dominate normal living humans was definitely not a good thing, even though the medieval Church was torturing and terrifying everyone in sight throughout Europe. It was okay for God to do this, but no one else could.

Vampires therefore provided a perfect mirror of the worst fears of the pious and perfect. Vampires were dangerous, sexually rampant, enormously powerful, absolutely unconcerned about human dignity and preservation of the soul, and finally . . . dead. And it was this last aspect of their nature that made them the most fascinating to legend-makers. They had overcome the one great stigma of life; that dark place which could never be explained. And therefore there was only one possible conclusion – they had to be grossly unhappy about it.

It was not until the gothic romantics of Byron's era that a few of the more imaginative writers decided that perhaps vampirism could be a desirable state, and even then, because of the Church's continued force, the pleasure of immortal sexual passion had ultimately to be destroyed by a stake in the heart. You could not afford to allow someone like Lord Ruthven to survive. He might after all eventually persuade too many people that being a vampire was just fine.

So if we delve back into the darkest shadows of vampiric history we find ourselves faced with just one phenomenon with which to begin – death.

Death Lies Bleeding

iven that man expresses his fear of wrongdoing through guilt, we can understand that primitive man might have understood his ability to kill through a fear that anything which he deprived of life might well come back to haunt him. If I slaughter an animal, I might be afraid that the animal will, in some way, take revenge upon me. I value life so much, after all. Worse, if I kill a human being, that departing soul will very likely take its revenge upon me by sucking my blood, the life-stuff of my existence.

So we might easily find the source of the vampire at the very outset of mankind's attempted comprehension of life and death. Primitive man would have observed his friend and family standing and moving around in life. He would then have observed the fact that the same people suddenly laid down and ceased movement. The body became static. But how could life suddenly stop? Surely something else simply replaced the body and continued to live in a place that was not visible? Thus the soul was born – invisible, elsewhere after life, and holy, because life was bad and difficult so therefore, by contrast, what happened after life must be good and easy – heaven.

But by contrast also, anything that could go to heaven must alternatively have the choice to go to hell, and in hell lay all the things that mankind considered unworthy of his fantasies – ideas that he dared not think of – forbidden fruits. And here lay the seed of the vampire, buried in unhallowed earth among all the dirt of unknown death.

Ancient tribes worshipped their dead as much as they did the gods. Especially kings were worshipped. But then mankind has still not lost that propensity, for kings, presidents, and even prime ministers are worshipped through the study of history, and the erection of statues today. We still maintain a reverence for the dead – may they rest in peace. And this is why the vampire myth has never died, for we feel respect for what happens after life, perhaps even more than we respect what happens in life.

And how many gods have required blood to be sacrificed to them? In order that the earth should continue to provide rich harvests, the blood of mankind should be spread across the ground. Mother Earth the vampire.

African tribes such as the Ovambo, who occupy the Bantu areas of South West Africa, will cut off the head and limbs of the dead in order to curtail the return of too many spirits into the world of the living. Their belief is that a careful spirit population control must be policed or trouble will follow. This may have been one of the earliest religious ideas to find its way into modern vampiric legend. One of the few foolproof methods of finishing off a vampire is to cut off its head and limbs. This way the spirit cannot "walk abroad," and cause trouble anymore.

The Caffre tribe believes that their dead may return and become rejuvenated by human blood, coming back from death specifically to drink the human liquid. Caffre living are horrified by dropped blood and will cover it on the ground, even if it falls from a bleeding nose or cut hand. The evil spirit might, after all, take up the single drop of blood and thereby reincarnate as something hideously evil.

Blood for almost all of the world's cultures has formed the very foundation for superstition and magic.

———————————◆———————————

Opposite – ritual magic and religion were intimately mixed in medieval Europe, with the devil being behind all evil and all dark mischief. His presence was a kind of reassurance that limits existed, beyond which humanity could not step.

For the life of the flesh is in the blood: therefore I said unto the children of Israel: You shall not eat the blood of any flesh at all, because the life of the flesh is in the blood, and whosoever eateth it, shall be cut off.

Animals had to be drained of blood before being eaten, and only the worst black magic cult practices would make use of the blood of creatures for their dark worship.

But with everything, there is always an opposite. Aboriginal tribes in Australia acknowledge the life-giving nature of blood for the living and make very little discrimination for the dead, believing that death is merely a step along the way. As part of their death rituals they will scratch the body of the deceased soon after death so that blood spills onto the ground. The idea is that the blood will give the deceased's soul a helping hand along the way to the next part of the trip. This most ancient of rituals would fit neatly into the concept that the dead need blood from the living.

Naming the Dead

At the end of the last chapter we made brief reference to the origin of the word "vampire." In many of the Mediterranean tongues the root, as we mentioned, came from the meaning "blood-monster." In other languages, such as those closer to Dracula's home, there are similar meanings in almost every language. The very earliest reference to the word arises in Slavonia in the Magyar form "vampir," which is the same in Russian, Polish, Czech, Serbian and Bulgarian, with some variations: "vapir," "vepir," "veryr," "vopyr," "upier."

In Lithuanian derivations there is an interesting variation on the idea of the vampire being not just a blood-monster but a blood-drunk. The word that gives rise to the idea of a vampire is a mixture of "wempti," meaning to drink, and "wampiti," to growl or mutter, and the use of the word gave an intonation of drunkenness. In Croatia the word for the vampire was "pijauica," meaning one who is red-faced with drink. In Albania the name for vampire means the restless dead, and in Greece and the surrounding territories there is no word for vampire at all.

In the European languages the name has always been somewhat similar: Danish and Swedish "vampyr," Dutch "vampir," French "le vampire," Italian, Spanish, Portuguese "vampiro," modern Latin "vampyrus." In the Oxford English Dictionary in its earlier editions the definition is:

A preternatural being of a malignant nature (in the original unusual form of the belief an animated Corpse), supposed to seek nourishment and do harm by sucking the blood of sleeping persons; a man or woman abnormally endowed with similar habits.

Ascending the Vampire Line

e speak now of the "Dark Ages" very simply because that's what they were. The records and systems of civilization set up by the Romans were destroyed after the end of the Empire and for 400 years Europe seems to have been plunged into darkness and chaos.

Many of the oldest traditions that had been around since Babylonian and Assyrian times were cultivated during these years, as magic became darker, witches became more powerful and monsters were seen on every corner. There were even carefully prepared qualifications for conditions under which the dead would rise again.

Whether thou art a ghost unburied,
Or a ghost that none careth for,
Or a ghost with none to make offerings to it,
Or a ghost that hath none to pour libations to it,
Or a ghost that hath no prosperity.
Or –
He that lieth in a ditch,
He that no grave covereth,
He that lieth uncovered,
Whose head is uncovered with dust,
The king's son that lieth in the desert,
Or in the ruins,
The hero whom they have slain with the sword.

Or –

He that hath died of hunger in prison,
He that hath died of thirst in prison,
The hungry man who in his hunger hath not smelt the smell of food,

He whom the bank of a river hath made to perish,
He that hath died in the desert or marshes,
He that a storm hath overwhelmed in the desert,
The Night-wraith that hath no husband,
The Night-fiend that hath no wife,
He that hath posterity and he that hath none.

It was tough not to be a vampire in those days!

The line of ascendency of the vampire is, in broad terms, easy to trace. If ever there was one vampire that has lived the whole span of tradition, he would need to be more or less 3,000 years old today. The peoples of the Assyrian and Babylonian empires were, as far as can be documented, the first to deal with difficult spirits and walking dead.

The same traditions of the "Ekimmu," the persistent haunters of ancient civilizations, survived into the Dark Ages and through into eastern Europe, where it is said to be still found today in countries such as Romania and Transylvania. The form of the monsters that range through the night, raping, sucking blood, and murdering, have even now, during the latter years of the twentieth century, found their way into American society where vampires are hardly documented at all in the ancient history of the country. The modern vampire is the serial killer who seduces innocent people into his home, defiles them in one way or another, murders, and then eats the body. Vampirism has truly hardly changed in over 3,000 years. The only real difference has been the ways in which the various cultures have dealt with the vampire and his friends.

In ancient Assyria incantations were used against any evil spirit that incarnated and took advantage of human flesh.

Spirits that minish heaven and earth,
That minish the land,
Spirits that minish the land,
Of giant strength,
Of giant strength and giant tread,
Demons like raging bulls, great ghosts,
Ghosts that break through all houses,
Demons that have no shame,
Seven are they!
Knowing no care,
They grind the land like corn;
Knowing no mercy.
They rage against mankind:
They spill their blood like rain,
Devouring their flesh and sucking their veins.
Where the images of the gods are, there they quake
In the Temple of Nabu, who fertilizes the shoots of wheat.
They are demons full of violence
Ceaselessly devouring blood.
Invoke the ban against them,
That they no more return to this neighborhood.
By heaven be ye exorcised! By earth be ye exorcised!

The beauty of death is here represented by a stone figure
in a mausoleum in Paris. Almost every graveyard in
Europe acts as a source of fear and horror.

The "Ekimmu" would be driven from the underworld by hunger and thirst, and when no offerings or sacrifices were made at the tomb, so the monster would partake of human flesh and blood instead. The same belief structure also existed in ancient Chinese mythology, particularly among Buddhists. And it is here that we find one of the origins of the idea that vampires can survive only at night. His dominion was believed to begin when the sun went for its rest, and the first rays of the morning drove him back into his grave. The very beginning of this superstition was, of course, the god of the sun himself, who had power over all of earth's activities, even to the extent of stopping home fires, making umbrellas potentially unlucky, and many other now forgotten capabilities (the old superstition related to opening an umbrella indoors was because the umbrella was originally used by priests only for protection against too much sun. It was known as a sun-wheel. To open the umbrella indoors was to insult the dominion of the sun).

But above all other fears existing throughout the ascendency of the undead, the one most frightening was that associated with the epidemic nature of vampiric attack. If the vampire sucked enough blood from his victim, so that victim became a vampire too.

The bubonic plague, known as "the pestilence" or "the black death," attacked Europe from the Far East during various disastrous periods of medieval history. It was the population leveler. It came to an area of the countryside as if like a dark, noxious wind, slaughtered thousands of hapless people in a matter of weeks and then floated away again. It was the greatest fear of the ages, and no one seemed able to do anything much about it. In the fourteenth century it is said to have killed around one third of the world's population, and the people of the time believed that it would wipe out mankind altogether before it left.

With such deeply rooted conditioning, the idea of pestilence and epidemic was strong in the medieval mind, and the creation of the vampiric legend relied for at least one of its characteristics on this.

It is interesting to note that many of the original characteristics of traditional vampirism seem to have arisen from China (as well as Assyria), and coincidentally so also did the first bubonic plague.

Far-Far East

In the Indian folktale *Vikram and the Vampire*, the monster is called the "Baital-Pachisi" and arises from an ancient Hindu origin. In the story, the hero *Raja* encounters the creature hanging upside-down in a very Indian style, from the branch of a tree.

It was

> *head downwards from a branch a little above him. Its eyes, which were wide open, were of greenish-brown, and never twinkled; its hair also was brown and brown was its face — these several shades which, notwithstanding, approached one another in an unpleasant way, as in an over-dried cocoa-nut. Its body was thin and ribbed like a skeleton or a bamboo framework, and as it held on to a bough, like a flying-fox, by the toe-tips, its drawn muscles stood out as if they were ropes of coir. Blood it appeared to have none, or there would have been a decided determination of that curious juice to the head; and as the Raja handled its skin, it felt icy cold and clammy as might a snake. The only sign of life was the whisking of a ragged little tail much resembling a goat's. Judging from these signs the brave king at once determined the creature to be a Baital — a Vampire.*

By contrast, in Malaysia vampires were designed to look more like gigantic mosquitoes, not unnaturally. The "Penanggalan" was a trunkless human head with a stomach hanging from the neck, which flew about sucking the blood of hapless victims, particularly children. By its description it might seem that it was specifically created to frighten children into behaving themselves and had no other existence than this.

Among the endlessly imaginative myths of the Far East there is another which brings us a kind of female vampire called the "Langsuior" who originally arose from a very beautiful woman who gave birth to a stillborn child and was so distressed that she transformed into the vampiric form, flew from where she stood, and remained for the rest of her life perched on trees. She wore always a green robe

and had tapering nails of extraordinary length (a mark of beauty in Malaysia), like talons. Her hair was long and jet black almost to her ankles and concealed a hole in the back of her neck through which she sucked the blood of children.

In the description from which we learn of this vampirish female there is something of a give-away as to the original source, insofar as the method advised by the writer for dealing with the "Langsuior" entails cutting off most of the tresses of hair, stuffing them into the hole in the back of her neck, and cutting off the long nails. The description of this method is completed with the following phrase:

> *...in which case she will become quiet and domesticated, just like an ordinary woman...!*

It maybe that the hole in the back of the neck was simply switched from the front, and the talons to be cut to the quick were a metaphor for the undomesticated woman's habit of making the writer's life difficult.

From this male chauvinist source came the female vampire, and the later European version of the superstition brought the story forward in a similar format:

> *If a woman dies in childbirth, either before delivery or after the birth of the child, and before the 40 days of uncleanness have expired, she is popularly supposed to become a "langsuyar," a flying demon of the nature of the "white lady" or "banshee." To prevent this a quantity of glass beads are put in the mouth of the corpse, a hen's egg is put under each armpit, and needles are placed in the palms of the hands. It is believed that if this is done the dead woman cannot become a "langsuyar," as she cannot open her mouth to shriek or wave her arms as wings or open and shut her hands to assist the flight.*

In Polynesia we find the "tu" or "talamaur," which eats chunks from his victims and then somehow becomes their "friend" or familiar. His favorite habit is to eat the flesh of a freshly dead person and thus absorb the final vitality from the body.

And finally, perhaps the most convincing source for the dark seat of the vampire legend is the West Indies, where vampirism was brought from what was earlier in the twentieth century known as Guinea and the Congo, and maintained by African slaves.

In Granada the vampire is called the "Loogaroo" and this unpleasant creature seems to have been born out of a hybrid of early French colonists' superstitions and the African voodoo that it came to destroy.

Loogaroos are human, especially female, who have made a pact with the devil by which they are given magical powers on condition that they provide their master with fresh warm blood each night. Each night, the loogaroo visits the "bombax ceiba" tree, an occult silk-cottontree also known in the region as the Devil's tree or the Jumbie tree. Once there, the loogaroo slips out of his skin, carefully folds it up and hides it under the tree or a nearby bush and then speeds about the local area on his ghastly task. Once the skin is taken off the loogaroo becomes concealed himself by turning his skinless body into a ball of sulphurous fire, and anyone visiting Granada even today will be taken from a house run by local people to be shown the darting fire of the loogaroo.

The only way to protect the home against the vampire is to spread rice and sand about the entrance. The loogaroo cannot enter the house until he has counted every grain, and will therefore be there till morning, when the sunlight will send him screaming back to the Devil's tree for his skin.

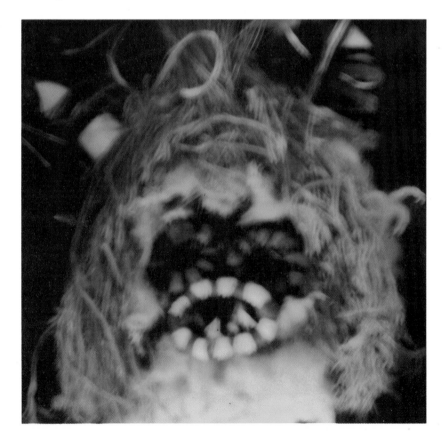

Chapter 8

How to kill a Vampire

ow does one kill fear, I wonder? How do you shoot a specter through the heart, slash off its spectral head, take it by its spectral throat? It is an enterprise you rush into while you dream, and are glad to make your escape with wet hair and every limb shaking. The bullet is not run, the blade not forged, the man not born; even the winged words of truth drop at your feet like lumps of lead. You require for such a desperate encounter an enchanted and poised shaft dipped in a lie too subtle to be found on earth. An enterprise for a dream, my masters!

How, indeed, do we kill our vampire once found, for we are still not sure whether it be a vision, a dream, a nightmare, or a glimpse into a reality "too subtle to be found on earth . . ."

Over the centuries, villagers have devised a number of methods which prevent corpses from becoming vampires, some of which we have seen already. They are numerous and often contradictory in practice from region to region, but tested countless times, and, for all the deaths that may have been caused by the monster, some have been spared with the observance of these techniques.

When all else fails, then one must kill, and following we give the methods which have been proven to work, eradicating the evil so that no more lives can be taken.

Both in prevention and in definitive action a series of steps must be taken and faithfully observed. Remember we are dealing with the forces of the supernatural and must therefore symbolically trespass the curtains of human experience and imbue ourselves with magical properties so that we may succeed in the enterprise. If vampires are creatures who dwell in midexistence, as we have proven they are, then we strike out in the same realm, and "the bullet is not run, the blade not forged, the man not born." And yet, vampires have been killed – or better said – they have been "given peace," since it is generally believed that the soul of the vampire is in a delirium, suffering, unable to extricate itself from the earthly, mortal knot which identifies our own existence here. Therefore the condition of vampirism is loathsome and tortuous to the vampire itself, and what better service could one render to the creature than the liberation of its soul?

Preventing the Dead

The methods of turning evil away and of preventing corpses from becoming vampires are many and diverse. Among them we may find mutilation of the corpse, physical restraint, curious funeral rites, and even deception intended to trick the spirit world.

One of the most widely used practices, which traces back to the antiquity of primitive man, is that of placing objects in the grave. These are believed to have the function of satisfying the corpse, of rendering it incapable of returning, and of satisfying or scaring away any evil force which may wish to interfere with it.

Coins were put inside the mouth of corpses in ancient Greece. With this gift the dead person could pay Charon the boatman for the passage across the River Styx, so that the soul would rest in peace after death.

In many regions of the world food is provided for the dead, because it is generally believed that the other world is similar to ours and that they need to eat. The belief is that food in the grave will prevent the corpse from feeding on the living. The foodstuffs may be both solid and liquid, drinks kept in jars and grains in bowls. Curiously, poppy seeds have often been found in burial grounds – possibly chosen for their apparent narcotic effect. This would encourage the dead to "sleep" rather than walk about in the land of the living.

The dead were thought to rise and attack passers-by. Bodies were carefully wrapped to prevent this.

In order to prevent potential vampires, in those regions where they were feared, from finding their way out of the grave, the deceased were often buried face down. They would not thus be able to see their way out of the coffin.

If the dead needed food the ancient mind reasoned they were in need of work also. In many agricultural villages the sickle, the archetypal symbol of reaping the harvest, was buried in the grave. This is possibly the origin of the portrayal of death as a skeleton carrying a sickle, as the "grim reaper" who takes lives.

Both food and work implements were intended to keep the corpse busy and satisfied so that there was no desire to return to the world of the living. These practices thus presuppose that all dead had a real desire to come back and be part of life again, and that unless specific measures were taken to prevent this from happening they would certainly return.

A useful device to keep potential vampires from sucking blood from the living was to insert a thorn under the tongue. No vampire likes to be pierced by his victim, though it is unlikely that, considering the vampire's enormous strength and hypnotic powers, the victim would get much of a chance to use the thorn.

Romania invented an "automatic vampire-piercing device" which consisted of one or several sharpened stakes, similar to those used by Prince Dracula for his impalements, driven into the grave so that when the body would seek to rise out of it, it would be automatically pierced and "killed" without the villagers needing to be on constant alert for a vampire insurgence.

In many instances skeletons have been found lying in their graves with their knees and/or wrists tied, and corpses, such as have been found in Bulgaria, rolled up inside a carpet. These were clear means of deterring *with force* the corpse from getting up and claiming victims from the nearby villages. The ropes that tied the limbs were hardly ever knotted since it was believed that the presence of knots in the grave would disturb the dead person's ability to make an easy transition to the afterlife.

Variations on funeral rites are a constant source of wonder. In one region of Romania, in Vrancea, it is said that it is unwise to cry over the dead. Instead, the family and friends must dance and sing so that any evil spirits in the vicinity will

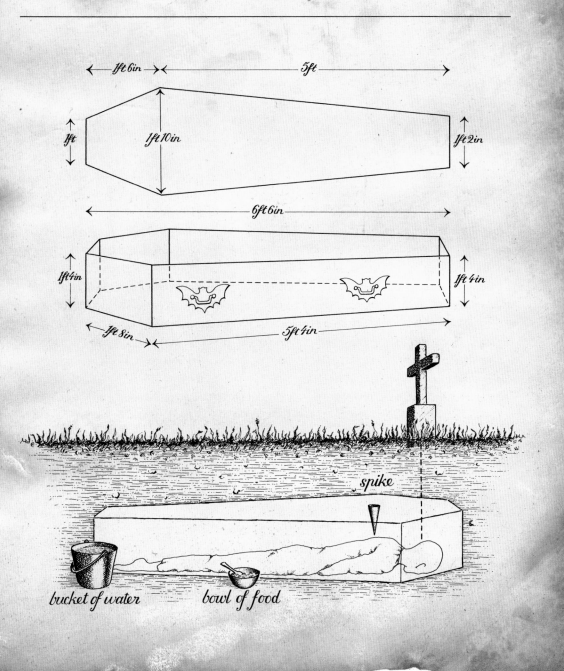

bucket of water
bowl of food
spike

imagine they are observing a festivity, not a burial. Sometimes, two men who are especially strong will take hold of the deceased and dance with him in the hope that the spirits in occupation will believe themselves not to be dead at all.

On the other hand, in southern Italy, Spain, and Greece, and in many other Catholic countries, it is ill-advised not to cry. Paid mourners are engaged to wail noisily behind the funeral procession so that the deceased feels he or she has been properly loved and missed and is thus not tempted to come back. Better off dead!

In antiquity and in such diverse regions as western Europe, Latin America and ancient Egypt, death was considered a slow process of transition from one state (life) to another (death). In societies where this is true, the burial, which occurs quickly after death, is temporary and provisional, and the funeral marks a long period during which a person is neither fully alive nor fully dead. During this period the corpse decomposes and the flesh decays until only the bones remain. This stage marks, in turn, rites of secondary burial during which the bones of the deceased are covered, ritually treated, and moved to a new location where they lie permanently stored.

It is the sites of first burial that struck most fear in the minds of the villagers and are mostly therefore set further away from the perimeter of the village than the secondary burial ground, to ensure that the spirits fail to find their way back home. It is believed that in the first instance, the dead are seeking to make the passage from this to the afterworld; this is a most delicate period since anything can disturb their transition and compel them to return to the land of the living.

In many cultures of the world, including our own, the buried body is weighed down with large blocks of rock. Our own tombstones, decorated with angels of peace, are a last remnant of this tradition, and the angel is intended to bring peace to the soul and to help it through the passage from death to the afterlife.

Many *natural* reasons have led people to believe that in the first burial grounds, the dead were not really dead at all. The phenomenon of *ignis fatuus*, or will-o'-the-wisp, seen so often at night burning over fresh graves is among them. The "little fire" was thought to be the flame of the soul still burning even after death, in much the same way as fairies appeared to humans in a transparent cloud

or as little flames dancing over the corollas of flowers at night. These two phenomena were taken for granted, and still are, and were in the same order of supernatural visitations from a world, unknown to us, but whose existence was parallel to ours. Now we know that a decomposing body produces great quantities of methane, a highly flammable gas, which mixes with other gases that ignite when surfacing above the ground to mix again with oxygen, which in turn ignites the methane.

The shifting of fresh graves was another, quite natural, phenomenon which convinced people that the dead were really not fully dead. There is a period of time during which the grave undergoes a certain amount of readjusting and settling, and cracks may appear on its rocky surface; this was taken as a sure sign that the dead were trying to escape from the burial site.

The secondary burial, on the other hand, was believed to be a place of peace since the dead had successfully completed their transition and were now not only at rest, but safely away from the human realm. Exhumations were carried out at the first burial posts, the remains burned, and the ashes placed within urns, a process very similar to the modern Southern European Catholic method of dealing with the remains of the dead.

In many modern cemeteries there is an organized way of moving around the remains as more space becomes available; exhumations are a matter of course, and after a suitable period, which may vary from seven to 20 years, the bones are taken out of the grave, burned, and the remains placed elsewhere. Is this practice simply due to practical reasons, or is it more to do with the rituals that have been undertaken without interruption since ancient Celtic times?

Many cemeteries in Italy also employ the practical habit of exhuming bodies after a period of time, breaking the remaining bones so that the body takes up less space and re-burying them in smaller coffins to save space. This too is no doubt related to the ancient practices.

It was during these exhumations that vampires were discovered. The natural expectation would have been to find a skeleton so that we might imagine the surprise that an undecomposed body would have afforded the cemetery caretakers.

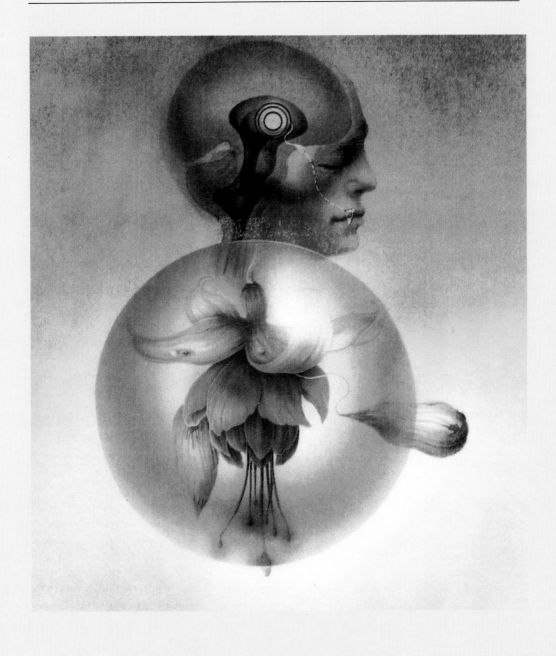

In order to prevent this from happening many cultures opted for the safe method of cremation. The bodies were cremated immediately after death and before burial to prevent the body from becoming a revenant and from returning to life. In fact, cultures who cremate their dead have never been afflicted by vampire epidemics. Cremation, however, is not such a simple matter, since the energy requirements for this process are high: an average "adult body weighing 160 lb. (73 kg.), cremated in a purpose-built furnace fired by gas, and with re-circulation of hot gases, is destroyed to ash in three-quarters to one hour of steady burning at a temperature around 1,600 F (870 C)." The total destruction of the body was thus in antiquity almost impracticable, and many wooden pyres, as throughout the Indian subcontinent, were coated with oil to provide a better combustion for the body, since the problem is not how big the fire is, but rather the ability to convey enough heat and for long enough to burn a body to ashes. In many countries, however, and especially in those villages afflicted by vampire epidemics, cremation was impractical and the villagers were thus forced by circumstances to bury the dead instead, thus risking their return.

Preventing the Vampire

If, despite all the measures taken to prevent the dead from becoming vampires, they are nevertheless born, then there are steps to prevent being attacked.

Various substances are deemed effective. Among these, garlic, the vampire chaser *par excellence*, is the most widely used. Vampires loath garlic and its smell is so detestable that they will never come near a house protected by it. Garlic was put in the grave as a preventative measure, but was also hung on the neck of the family of the deceased, hung around rooms, especially around windows, doors and on bedheads. It was also rubbed onto door and window-frames and even on farm animals to prevent an attack.

The use of garlic was adopted to fence off all epidemics. Both in the plague years and during a vampire insurgence people added garlic to their diets and wore "necklaces" made of it. The highly commendable properties of garlic form a natural antibiotic and its use in food makes for a healthy diet.

As we have seen already, there are many similarities between the plague and a vampire epidemic, for the latter was believed to be "catching" like a terminal virus. The bad smell, the "smell of death," associated with the plague was believed to be the cause of the illness since its true origin had not yet been discovered. In order to safe-guard themselves from it, the population used strong smelling substances in the belief that these were a good antidote to bad smells. Garlic was one of these, except that its health-enhancing properties were the true medicine. Wolfsbane is another herb widely used, and this was hung or used in the same way or in conjunction with garlic. Silver knives were placed under mattresses and cribs to further strengthen the anti-vampire barrier.

Feature films on vampires have spread the belief that the creatures fear the crucifix. However, there is scarcely any evidence that this is so, either in folklore or in the fiction dealing with the subject. The Church and God have, unfortunately, little to do with vampirism in truth, excepting perhaps that some prayers might help the dead from returning, and suitable formulas are recited at the funeral to help the soul find its peace. There is no more effective method to ban vampirism than killing.

Killing the Vampire

he classic, well-tested method of killing a vampire is to drive a stake through its heart. The dramatic possibilities of this situation have always been irresistible to writers and film directors. The vampire is portrayed as lying in its coffin dressed beautifully in a tuxedo, the courageous vampire killer drives a stake through its heart, and then pounds on it with a mallet. The vampire's features are contorted by pain and the eyes transfixed in a hateful state. The creature screams, and suddenly hundreds of years appear on the face until it crumbles to dust or becomes a mummified corpse.

The process of staking is not as simple as it might appear in the hammer horror movies. An old piece of fencing or whittled chair leg will not do. In Russia and throughout the Baltic area, for instance, the appropriate wood for the purpose is ash, for its magical properties. In Silesia, on the other hand, such stakes were carved from oakwood, and in Serbia from hawthorn because of its thorny shrub properties – vampires are highly allergic to thorns.

In the absence of a stake, vampires have been known to be killed with a silver dagger, although the operation proves more difficult, and the majority of stories concerning the silver dagger seem more likely to be associated with the killing of werewolves – a subject needing another complete volume to examine. A stake driven with force at the center of the heart is by far the best and most successful method.

The bloating of the bodies in the grave, proof of vampire takeover, was seen as an attempt of the soul, or whatever had taken possession, to escape. The piercing of the stake would have provided a good way out. Certainly the vampire killers can clearly see that *something* is escaping when they pierce a decomposing body.

In some accounts of vampire killings we learn that after the piercing of the body had taken place, the blood gushed high into the air. This can be explained by the pressure in the body built up by all the gases produced in decomposition.

The famous vampire-groan which occurs after the stake has pierced the heart is due to the lungs being compressed by the attack and the air and gases being forced rather explosively through the trachea, producing, quite understandably, a shriek not unlike a cry of terror from a living person. It may be, however, that the vampire genuinely groans as its soul attains the much longed-for liberation. There is invariably both a scientific as well as a good irrational explanation, and no reason to suppose that either one is false . . . or true.

A number of additional steps can be taken after staking the dread creature. The heart can be cut out, burned, and its ashes scattered in the waters of a flowing river. In 1874 a Romanian prince settled in Paris after being forced into exile because the members of his family were believed by their compatriots to turn into vampires at death. The young prince cut out his open heart while he was dying to prevent himself from turning into a vampire.

Some people cover the vampire with a shroud or a piece of cloth before doing anything to it, in case the blood spills over them and transforms them into vampires too.

———————•———————

Lands where vampires walk the dread night are many in Scotland. Opposite are the forests beside Loch Flynne in Argyleshire.

For the super-neurotic, all or several of these remedies may be undertaken together, often resulting in a terrible and gory mess. So we find that sometimes not only is the heart cut out, burned, and thrown into water, but the head is chopped off, the corpse reburied at a crossroads, and the coffin filled with poppy seeds and other magic charms. Every possibility is covered to make really sure that the vampire is killed.

In the case of a vampire plague in France, the Pope was forced to consecrate the River Rhone so that bodies could be thrown into it without delay, when the churchyard was no longer sufficient.

Additional killing by fire and by water are thus considered two good measures after the staking to ensure the end of vampirism.

Who is to be the killer? It is said that the killer should be motivated, since a person seeking revenge is more likely to sustain the terror and fright until final death is accomplished. A vampire who has only been half-killed because the killer has run away in panic is a thousand-fold more dangerous than an ordinary vampire. Countless men, whose fiancees were bled to death by the evil creatures, form the main corpus of the vampire hunters and killers. Sometimes, however, it is the victim who gathers enough courage to kill the beast who is slowly but surely sucking her life, and, after the killing is over, the victim must smear the bites on her neck with the blood that has ensued from the dead body, as it is really her own blood flowing in someone else's veins and this act is the only cure to heal the bites.

Acknowledgments

The publishers would like to thank the following contributors to the book. Whilst every effort has been made to trace all present copyright holders of this material, any unintentional ommission is hereby apologized for, and we shall correct any errors in acknowledgments in any future edition of this book.

ALLIED ARTISTS 2, 6, 64, 155, 159, 160. BFI STILLS, POSTERS AND DESIGNS 77, 100, 141, 164, 173, 179. COLORIFIC PHOTO LIBRARY LTD. 190, 191. DIANA AND MARLO 10/11. DUDLEY YEO 81, 102, 103. FRANK SPOONER 168. GARY WOODS 207. GILLIAN NEWMAN 69, 79, 89, 110, 111, 213. JOHN GAY/JOHN MURRAY 72, 85, 142, 148, 167, 211, 215. MARY EVANS PICTURE LIBRARY 15, 156. RAYMOND PIAT/GAMMA 32, 33. SIMON MARSDEN/THE MARSDEN ARCHIVE 18, 26, 27, 29, 34, 36, 49, 55, 56, 58, 59/60, 67, 86, 95, 115, 119, 120, 123, 124, 139, 151, 166, 182, 193, 202, 205, 218, 222. SUSAN GRIGGS 90/91, 116. THE IMAGE BANK 176, 177. © 1932 TURNER ENTERTAINMENT CO. ALL RIGHTS RESERVED 43. PICTOR INTERNATIONAL 104, 105. WELLCOME INSTITUTE LIBRARY, LONDON 145, 185, 186. YOUNG ARTISTS 71, 108. ZEFA 40, 52, 53, 113, 132/133, 147, 152/153, 208/209.